JUST LIKE JACK

Other Available Books by Shirley Marks:

Lady Eugenia's Holiday
His Lordship's Chaperone
An Agreeable Arrangement
Miss Quinn's Quandary
Honeymoon Husband
Geek to Chic

JUST LIKE JACK

•

Shirley Marks

AVALON BOOKS
NEW YORK

Published by Thomas Bouregy & Co., Inc.
160 Madison Avenue, New York, NY 10016

Library of Congress Cataloging-in-Publication Data

Marks, Shirley.
Just like Jack / Shirley Marks.
    p. cm.
ISBN 978-0-8034-7774-2
1. Best friends—Fiction.   I. Title.
PS3613.A7655J87 2010
813'.6—dc22
                        2010006237

PRINTED IN THE UNITED STATES OF AMERICA
ON ACID-FREE PAPER
BY HADDON CRAFTSMEN, BLOOMSBURG, PENNSYLVANIA

To Nadine and Jim for sharing their family

Chapter One

Megan Donnelly helped herself to an eyeful of Jack when he leaned into her refrigerator to help himself to a can of ginger ale. Jack Meredith had the most dazzling brown eyes and the best smile she'd ever seen.

He had never shown the least bit of interest in her—ever. She suspected he probably couldn't see beyond her role as Eric's-little-kid-sister, but it hadn't stopped them from being best friends. And it didn't stop her from using him as the standard for every guy she dated.

"My mother called again. She wants to hear all about the *girlfriend* I'm bringing to my sister's wedding." Jack popped the tab to open the can and flashed a self-conscious smile.

Girlfriend? Uh-oh. "You mean your mom wants details? Like what she looks like, how long you've known her, her name?" Megan gave him the please-continue look. She was going to get the whole story because that's what best buds did for each other—listen.

"I think she's expecting a significant other."

"So you need to find a willing girl?"

"*Woman*—please." He cringed. "*Girl* sounds like a

1

twelve-year-old. Besides, I know just the woman I need." Jack gave her a don't-play-dumb-with-me-you-know-what-I'm-talking-about look.

Megan's breath caught in her throat. "You want *me* to go with you?"

Jack took a swig of ginger ale. "Who else can I turn to? You know the wedding is next weekend; I gave you fair warning months ago."

But Megan never thought he'd meant to bring her.

"You know you'll be perfectly safe with me," he stated, reassuring her of his sincerity.

Unfortunately, yes. "I guess we'd have to pretend to be *involved.*"

"I guess we *could,*" he mimicked, happily and all bright-eyed.

Acting lovey-dovey with Jack wouldn't take any pretending on her part. She could just imagine how good it would feel to be held tightly in his arms.

Megan rubbed her hands together, erasing the imagined vision of touching the crispness of his white shirt, and gave herself a mental shake. Helping him out would probably be a bad idea.

But a small part of her brain tiptoed off and wondered how it would feel to run her fingers through his soft, wavy brown locks.

A very bad idea, the sensible part of her said.

Jack shoved one of his shirtsleeves to his elbow and sank into a kitchen chair, waiting for an answer.

"Hold it." Megan sat across the table from him. "Can I think about this for a minute?"

"What's to think about? If you're in trouble, I help you. If I'm in trouble, you help me. I guarantee, if I show up without a date, my mother will find one for me. And that's—"

"Unthinkable," Megan finished for him.

"The absolute worst."

This was crazy. Why even consider masquerading as his girlfriend? Then the answer came to her. Because Jack had asked. He was right: he was in trouble. She couldn't say no.

"Let's see if I understand this right. We show up at your parents' house, spend the weekend pretending to be the perfect couple, and when we get home—boom—it's splitsville? What are you going to tell your family about our breakup?"

Jack choked. "B-Breakup?" His tone was heart-wrenching.

They weren't really breaking up. What was she thinking? They weren't even together . . . as a couple.

"You know what I mean." She gave him a hard stare, knowing he knew exactly what she meant.

"I guess I'll have to tell them it didn't work out and we've gone back to being just friends."

Megan crossed her arms and stared at him, wondering if doing him a favor now would really be doing her any favors.

The door buzzer sounded.

"That's probably Leslie." Megan got up from the table and headed for the door.

"The one-you-work-with Leslie?" he guessed, and he stood with her.

"The one and only."

"You two going shopping?" Jack followed her and rested against the back of the sofa.

"No, the movies." Megan opened the door. "Come on in." Leslie stood there and stared. Her eyes twinkled, and a slow smile began to spread across her face. "Leslie, have you met Jack?"

Leslie sauntered up to him and held out her hand. "No, I'm afraid I've never had the pleasure."

"Jack's my neighbor—he lives across the hall," Megan told her, but she wasn't sure Leslie heard a single word.

Jack shook her hand. "Nice to meet you, Leslie. I'll leave you two ladies to your afternoon. I was on my way out anyway." He handed the half-empty soda can to Megan and headed for the door.

Megan couldn't believe Leslie. She was practically drooling.

"Don't forget to mark your calendar," Jack said over his shoulder. "The wedding is Saturday, May 20. We'll be flying to Des Moines on Thursday, the eighteenth, and returning on the following Sunday, the twenty-first." He started to pull the door closed behind him.

"Wait a minute!" Megan called out. "I never said yes."

The door swung back open, and Jack poked his head back into the room and grinned. "You didn't say no either."

Jack closed his apartment door behind him, sank into his reclining chair, and turned on the TV with the remote. Talk about mixed signals. Jack knew Megan liked him; he was sure of it.

Click. Channel 23 . . . classic cartoons.

Click. Channel 24 . . . wild animals.

Sure, they were friends. Best friends. He and Megan got along great.

Click. Channel 25 . . . some reality show with twenty-somethings behaving badly.

Click. Channel 26 . . . an old black-and-white movie.

Why were things so sluggish in the romance department?

Click. Channel 27 . . . music videos.

Click. Channel 28 . . . World War II warplanes in action.

Jack didn't even want to think about any other woman except Megan. Jack and Megan. Megan and Jack.

Click. Channel 29 . . . lawyers discussing legal cases.

Click. Channel 30 . . . the space channel.

Jack stared at the rotating Earth as seen from the orbiting space shuttle, and he zoned out.

He hadn't always been in love with Megan. He hadn't known it the first time he met her ten years ago. He hadn't known it nine months ago when he moved in across the hall from her. But she wasn't Eric Donnelly's little sister anymore. It had been a shock to see her once-long, straight, dark brown hair swinging in a sassy, chin-length bob.

Jack hadn't known he was totally in love with Megan until eight months, two weeks, six days, four hours, and twenty-seven minutes ago, give or take a few seconds. And he knew the instant it happened. The very instant.

Standing in her apartment, Megan had loosened a chocolate chip cookie off a cookie sheet she had pulled out of the oven. She'd looked at him and asked, "Do you want this?"

And—*boom*—that was the moment. When their gazes met. That look in her eyes. That's when it all jelled—her warmth, her tenderness. He wanted no other woman but her, Megan, forever.

Mission control splashed across the screen. Jack blinked, coming out of his cosmic spell, and sat up.

Click. Channel 31 . . . cooking competition. From the looks of it, they were waiting for water to boil.

Click. Channel 32 . . . hip-hop videos.

Give her time; she's young yet. She was still playing the field.

Click. Channel 33 . . . some guy digging in a garden, or was it the back forty?

Megan needed to sow her wild oats.

Click. Channel 34 . . . interior-design tips.

That is, if women had wild oats to sow.

Click. Channel 35 . . . the television shopping channel.

If he was wrong about how much she liked him, if she couldn't make the leap over the just-friends line . . . he might lose the *wonderful* they had now.

Click. Channel 36 . . . a soap opera . . . in Spanish . . . and no subtitles. Still, it was clear that the couple on the screen wasn't getting along. It was more than that—a lover's quarrel. The woman was in tears, and the guy . . . well, he stood there like an idiot.

"Don't let her cry!" Jack told the guy. "You love her. I know you do."

The guy hadn't moved an inch. All he did was give the woman a soulful, intense look.

"Tell her," Jack urged. "Tell her!"

The guy finally listened to Jack and told her. She fell into his arms, and they ended the scene with a kiss in time for the credits to roll.

Jack smiled and nodded. "That's right. I told you it'd work." He completely believed that the right guy at the right time made all the difference.

In Megan's case, the right time was soon, and the right guy, he vowed, was going to be him.

"Him!" Leslie jabbed her finger in the direction Jack had gone. "Where have you been hiding *him*? *Why* would you hide him?"

"I haven't been *hiding* him, Les." Megan laid that morning's newspaper on the kitchen counter.

"I don't understand. You've been on a worldwide search for Mr. Right. What about him, Jack? He's perfect."

"Don't I wish." Jack was perfect in every way except the most important one—being a willing participant.

"Why didn't you date him instead of Steven the Sponger?"

"Steven was *not* a sponger." Megan didn't understand her need to defend him. Steven had been her last boyfriend, but he was long gone; they'd broken up months ago.

"I don't know about you, but when a man asks you out and expects you to pick up the tab—that would make me wonder." Leslie's tone had turned sarcastic.

"He forgot his wallet," Megan reminded her.

"*Every* time you went out?"

"We didn't go out that much."

Leslie set her purse on the coffee table and settled on the arm of the sofa. "You can say that again."

Megan didn't even want to think about the last two weeks she and Steven were together. It was too depressing.

"Yeah," Leslie continued. "Good thing you have cable television. All you did was watch TV."

"I like watching TV," Megan mumbled. She didn't need to hear it from Leslie; Megan knew where this conversation was going. Where it always went. Why did she always pick losers?

"The war channel?" Leslie slipped into a baritone announcer's voice. "Experience war in real time. World War I, World War II, war every day, all day, twenty-four hours a day. It took you forever to toss the Sponger's two-ton cannon out of here."

"Watching TV isn't so bad," Megan replied. Again, why the need to defend Steven? It had taken her only a couple of weeks to figure out that he was a freeloader. "I watch TV with Jack too. We watch the Explorer Channel."

A smile crossed Leslie's lips, and she swung her crossed leg. "I'd like to explore Jack." She drummed her fingers on her knee. "How much of that magnificent man is there? He's got to be at least six feet tall."

"Jack says six-one."

"Those broad shoulders make him look even taller . . . bigger."

"I know." Megan sighed, feeling a little woozy herself.

Leslie sighed too. Her eyes grew as dreamy as her voice. "What does he do? Oh, please tell me he's rich, and if you're going to take him, please tell me he has a brother."

"Sorry. He's got two sisters. He works at a place called TriLogic. It's one of those start-up companies, you gold digger."

"Oh, well." Leslie tossed her hair over her shoulders. "It's nice to know these things up front."

Megan didn't know how much Jack made and would never tell Leslie even if she knew. But he'd never asked to borrow money from her, unlike other ex-boyfriends who would remain nameless.

"How about if we skip the movie and drill a hole in the wall to see if we can get a closer peek at him?"

"Excuse me, Jack lives *across* the hall," Megan clarified, pointing out the futility of a peephole.

"You like him. I know you do."

Megan hoped her stifled smile wasn't giving her away.

"Don't try to deny it." Leslie sat forward, pinning her with a stare. "Come on. What's really wrong with him?"

"Forget it, will you?" Megan turned the newspaper to the movie section. "What were we going to see?"

"How about *Salads with Stud Muffins on the Side*?"

Megan ignored her. "Can't find it. Must have missed it. How about the new Pamela Austen flick? What's it called?" She scanned the theater listings, hoping a title would ring a bell.

"*Total Denial*?" Leslie ventured. "Come on." She slapped her hand in the middle of the paper, stopping Megan from reading further. "You've got to have a really good reason for not going after him, because it seems like Jack is the perfect man."

There was no use. Leslie wasn't going to quit prodding until she knew everything. "No, Leslie," Megan said.

"There's nothing wrong with him. It's just that Jack is the ultimate bachelor."

"That's too bad. He's one of the . . . unattainable." Leslie went a little pale, reached for a kitchen chair, and eased into it. "You can date them, but you can't *have* them. He's so gorgeous. And those dimples are to die for."

"They just kill you, don't they? You should see him smile." Megan understood completely. Jack *was* the perfect guy. "He was my brother Eric's college roommate. Eric brought Jack home for semester break one year. I was a sophomore in high school, and he was gorgeous. When I first saw him smile, those dimples turned me into a puddle. And I'm sure he never even knew I was alive."

"From the sound of it, he doesn't know now."

"I know. I never got that *interested* vibe from him."

"Maybe he's using you as an estrogen fix until he hooks up with his next girlfriend."

"I'll tell you, Les, the memory of that smile and those dimples have kept me going for the last ten years."

"They're fantasy kindling, if you ask me. It's a real shame. All that man going to waste." Leslie sounded less than enthusiastic.

"Well, he's over here a lot, dinner at least two or three times a week. I love having him around. I just wish . . ." Megan shrugged. Jack was kind and thoughtful, funny and sensitive. If there were something she could do to get him to notice her, she'd do it. As things were . . . "It doesn't matter. He just wants to be friends. He has no romantic interest in me at all. I've seen the women he dates. He likes tall blonds, and I'm a short brunette."

"So you're not his type. That is truly a shame." By the sound of Leslie's voice, Megan guessed the message had finally been received loud and clear: nothing was ever going to happen between her and Jack.

"Spending time with Jack is great, but I think he's spoiling me. The guys I meet don't measure up. I haven't had a decent date in—"

"What do you call *going away with him*?" Leslie asked, wide-eyed. "That sounds promising."

"It's not a date. He hasn't had a girlfriend in six months. He needs someone to go with to his sister's wedding, and I'm supposed to save him from his matchmaking mother."

Chapter Two

After the movie with Leslie, Megan stopped at the grocery store on her way home. She checked her purse, then her jeans pockets, front and back, for her shopping list. The only thing she found was a wadded tissue. She'd have to shop by memory. Again.

Swinging by the frozen-food section, she picked up a carton of ice cream to help her forget about her sagging love life. Then she remembered she didn't have any room in the freezer and returned the carton to the shelf. She really should spend some time cleaning out her refrigerator.

Megan turned down the breakfast-food aisle in search of milk, orange juice, and cereal. Another shopping cart squeezed in front of her, cutting her off.

"Hey, watch where you're going, lady," said a silly-sounding but familiar voice.

"Jack? What are you doing here?"

"A guy's got to eat." Jack held up a box of cereal. "I'm all out of Cheerios."

"You've been out of cereal for a month and mooching off me ever since."

"Oh, sorry. Here." He set the box of cereal in her cart.

"I prefer the multigrain, if you please."

"I can adapt. There's no such thing as bad cereal." Jack handed Megan another box, her multigrain choice this time. "I'm not kidding. Did you know that we're throwing Cheerios at my sister's wedding?"

Megan stared at him.

"Just kidding—Rice Krispies, really. We are, I swear." He held up his right hand and placed his left on the cereal box in Megan's hand.

Megan glanced skyward, thinking him unbelievable, and continued down the shopping aisle.

Jack kept pace at her side. "Are you ready to go off into the wilds of Iowa?"

"I wouldn't miss a chance to throw breakfast cereal at a wedding." Megan picked up a quart of orange juice and a quart of milk and set them in her basket.

"Do you think you'll have any problem getting off from work Thursday and Friday?" Jack reached into Megan's cart, picked up the quart of milk, and replaced it on the refrigerated shelf. He set a gallon container of milk in her basket. "I'm sorry this is such short notice."

"Like you said, you gave me fair warning. You told me months ago that Shelley was getting married, and I should have dusted off my wedding attire just in case I needed to stand in."

"And that's all you have to do. You don't really have to pretend to be my girlfriend." He looked away, appearing almost embarrassed by the notion.

"I don't?" Megan would have thought that that was exactly what he wanted—for his mother's sake.

"That was just a joke. Oh, look, Ovaltine." He leaned in front of her, reaching for a brown glass bottle, his face a scant inch from hers. "I haven't had that since I was a kid. You've got to try some of this."

Megan closed her eyes. Maybe if she didn't see him, she could ignore him. She couldn't hear his soft, shallow breathing, she told herself. She couldn't smell the ever-so-slight tang of his aftershave or feel the warmth of his cheek on her lips.

Oh, forget it. She felt the attraction to him; every inch of her buzzed. If only he could feel it too.

Megan sensed Jack straighten and move away. He held a container with the label toward her. She blinked, trying to focus on the words or at least the logo of the product.

"Ovaltine. Great stuff." He set it in his cart and pushed it forward.

Megan stayed behind to catch her breath and tried to regroup her scattered thoughts. All she could think of was Jack.

"You're out of this too." Jack curled his index finger through the handle of a maple syrup bottle. "I used the last of it this morning." He turned around and set it in Megan's cart.

He'd had pancakes in her apartment that morning.

"Look, fruit gummies! I have to have some of those." He pulled his cart to one side and leaned over to check out the assortment of gummy bears, gummy sharks, and various other gummy-type fruit snacks in assorted animal shapes on a lower shelf.

Megan could not help herself. Wasn't he adorable?

Was she crazy? Why did she torture herself? How did she think she could remain sane being alone with Jack for four whole days?

Jack set a box of the gummies in his shopping cart. Megan tightened her grip on the handle of hers and pushed forward to the checkout line. He pulled up behind her.

Megan glanced into his basket. "Why do you bother shopping at all?"

He picked up his Ovaltine and gummies, allowing a store clerk to take his empty basket. "Like I said, a guy's got to eat."

"But you eat *my* food." Megan wasn't really complaining, just trying to make a point. Her grocery bill had grown in proportion to the length of time Jack had lived across the hall.

The line moved forward.

"I only eat half."

She stared at him, waiting for the rest of it. Because, knowing Jack, there was more to follow.

"Okay, I'll cut you a deal. If I eat half, I think the least I can do is pay half, but this time"—he flipped open his wallet and handed her some bills—"it's on me."

Fair was fair. Megan took the twenties. Jack tossed his stuff into her cart. "If we had planned ahead, you could've saved yourself a trip to the store, or at least we could have carpooled."

Jack took the gallon of milk and quart of orange juice from Megan's shopping cart and set them behind the Ovaltine, box of gummies, and the three boxes of cereal they'd collected between them. The checkout belt rotated, moving their groceries closer to the cashier.

"What did you get *us* for dinner tonight?" Jack gave Megan's items a quick once-over.

"*We're* having chicken with roasted potatoes and a salad," she reported.

"You didn't get any ice cream," he complained.

"We still have some caramel crunch from the other night."

"Good afternoon, Megan. Jack." Nancy, the cashier, greeted them. She looked from Megan to Jack, showing mild surprise. "Are you two together?"

Did Nancy mean personal-wise or grocery-wise?

Jack answered matter-of-factly, "Yes, we're together."

Sounded as if they were an old married couple. But no matter how much Megan wished that were true, it could never be. Not today. Not tomorrow. Not ever.

"May I have your attention please?" Leslie's voice boomed over the warehouse PA system the next day at work. "Megan Donnelly promises to go out with every man who comes up to the front office within the next five minutes."

Megan yanked the microphone out of Leslie's hands by its thick, curly cord. "What do you think you're doing?"

"I think it's time for desperate measures." Leslie readjusted her blouse.

"Desperate—" Megan drew in a slow, controlled breath, resisting the urge to strangle her co-worker with the cord. "You're crazy, you know that? And I'm not desperate."

"Well, you should be."

"What's that supposed to mean?"

"Point being . . . one, you're not currently dating."

"I don't have to date," Megan replied. She'd been without a steady boyfriend for a couple of months, and she was managing quite nicely.

"Two, when you do, you always pick the wrong guy."

Megan had to agree with Leslie that finding someone like Jack would not be easy. Up until the present it had proved impossible.

"And announcing free dates over the PA system is going to attract the *right* kind of guy?" Megan shook her head. "We're definitely *not* on the same wavelength here." She hung up the microphone and headed back to her desk.

"What's the big deal, anyway? There's no one in the warehouse; they're all out to lunch. I was trying to give my argument some impact."

"But what if someone had heard you?"

"Relax—you worry too much." Leslie eased back into her chair.

"There's nothing wrong with *not* seeing anybody." Megan did not expect Miss I'm-Never-without-a-Boyfriend to understand why she was unattached at the moment.

The only reason Megan dated a lot of men was in hopes of finding someone like Jack. But making a cattle call was just cruel. Leslie was supposed to be her friend—except friends weren't supposed to make you feel worse. They were supposed to boost your spirits.

"The point I want to make is . . . you don't have a problem attracting guys. It means you need to change your tactics and attract a different *kind* of guy."

"Like *your* kind of guy?"

"They don't pick me; I pick them," Leslie was very quick to point out. And she had. Leslie always got her man—a man of her choosing.

So maybe Megan didn't have a great record when it came to men. And maybe, just maybe, she could use some men tips from Leslie the Discriminating.

"Isn't it obvious?" Leslie was going to offer up her observations.

Megan thought back to some of her own recent failures: Kevin the Conniver, always on the lookout for his next babe; Greg, who always traveled with his personal green-eyed monster, jealous of everyone—including the non-threatening Jack Meredith. Then she recalled the recently discussed Steven the Sponger.

"Well, okay. So I haven't been able to come close to finding a guy like Jack."

"I don't think you've even moved the needle on the Ultimate Man meter." Leslie leaned forward. "It's still sitting on the big fat zero."

What hurt Megan the most was that Leslie was right. She probably couldn't pick a decent guy if he were growing on a tree in the middle of her living room. They all seemed like nice, decent men when she first met them, but, after she'd spent some time with them, they seemed to change, and not for the better.

That she had managed to see their bad side within a matter of weeks was really a total blessing.

"You'll also notice, we aren't getting much of a response." Leslie's pointed comment smarted a bit.

"What did you expect from an empty warehouse?" Megan shrugged, pretending it was funny.

A knock sounded. Megan froze and glared at Leslie, who apparently was just as shocked. Leslie shrugged, muffled her laughter, and headed for the door.

"So help me, Leslie . . ." Megan didn't need to fake her anger. Once they were alone, she was going to strangle her co-worker.

Leslie pulled the door open, stepped back, and flashed Megan a wicked smile before greeting their guest. "Hello, there," she purred in a way that said dishy-man alert. "Mr. Right, isn't it?"

Chapter Three

*M*r. *Right, knocking at the door?*

"Brandon Wright, West Coast rep for Allied Federated. We met last Tuesday."

Megan couldn't see him, but his voice was deep and dreamy.

"Mr. Wright, of course. Please come in." Leslie pulled the door wide open, and he stepped in.

Leslie's usual conception of Mr. Right was a six-foot-four version of a Hollywood leading man with the brainpower of a Brussels sprout. Just looking at *this* guy made Megan's stomach do flip-flops. He was tall, blond, tan, and clearly frequented a gym.

"Call me Brandon, please," he said.

Megan hated to agree with Leslie about a man, but . . . he was so gorgeous and really, really smooth.

He turned his beautiful baby blues on Megan. "I don't believe I've had the pleasure."

"I'm . . . I'm . . ." Megan stammered and glanced at Leslie, hoping for her memory to reappear.

"Megan Donnelly. *Miss* Megan Donnelly," Leslie supplied.

"Yes, that's it, Megan Donnelly," Megan repeated, holding her hand out. "Nice to meet you."

"You're here to see Kay Rogers, aren't you?" Leslie was cooking up something. "Megan can take you down to Kay's office." She shoved Megan toward Brandon. "It's just down the hall."

Megan stopped short of colliding with the man. She stepped into the corridor and paused, waiting for him to catch up.

"Megan Donnelly, huh?" His broad smile and the glimmer in his eyes told Megan that he was interested in her as more than just a guide. Even the way he said her name sounded flirtatious.

"That's right." If only Jack looked at her that way.

Gazing into Brandon's eyes, it occurred to her that maybe Jack didn't have to. Maybe Brandon Wright would be the one to get her over her infatuation with Jack.

"So, Megan Donnelly, you seem like a nice girl."

"I'd like to think so." They passed the Human Resources area and continued toward Finance on their way to the Purchasing department.

"Well, I think so too." He came to a halt, which made Megan stop to wait for him. "So tell me, do you date company employees?"

"No, I don't." If she did, that would be asking for trouble right there.

He nodded, apparently liking that answer. "What about outside vendors?" Brandon watched her closely.

"I've never had the opportunity." She couldn't help smiling. Did he want to ask her out?

"And if you had the opportunity, would you?" There was something about the way he watched her. As if she meant something important to him. But that couldn't be; they'd only just met.

"It depends. I'd have to give it some thought." Megan didn't want to rush into anything.

"How about you think about it over dinner tonight? Chez Louis—how's that sound?"

That sounded pretty good. Her smile widened. Her heart was beating in double time. Why was she feeling like this?

"I've got a late meeting, but I can pick you up at nine."

They didn't need to have dinner tonight. What was the rush?

"Or I can meet you there at eight, if you'd like. What do you say?" He pinned her with a bright, optimistic stare that she found hard, if not impossible, to refuse.

What the heck? "All right. Chez Louis it is, eight o'clock."

Fifteen minutes after Megan had left her office, she returned to an eager Leslie. How had the woman known that Brandon Wright would ask Megan out, anyway?

"Well?" Leslie wanted to hear all the details.

Megan managed a nod even though her head still felt a little woozy.

"Nice move, girl." Leslie clapped Megan on the shoulder. "Now he's what I call a good choice."

The long string of losers Megan had dated had never made her forget Jack, but this guy was different. Megan thought for the first time that Brandon Wright just might.

Jack returned home after a long day at work. He strolled down the hall to his apartment, and, as he always did, he knocked on Megan's front door to announce, "Hi, Meg, I'm home."

"Jack! Wait!" she cried out. "Come in!"

Jack stepped inside. No Megan. "Meg? Megan? Where are you?"

"I'm in the bedroom. Wait right there, will you? I'll be out in a minute."

"What's going on?" Jack set his briefcase next to the door. He loosened his tie and undid the top button of his shirt on his way to the refrigerator.

"I've got a date tonight, and I need a second opinion," Megan called from the back.

Jack didn't like the sound of her voice—it was too perky. This was the first time he'd had to do a wardrobe check before she went out. Another bad sign.

Snagging a can of ginger ale, Jack straightened and stared toward Megan's bedroom. No, he didn't like anything about this at all. He wiped the rim of the can with his finger a couple of times before popping it open.

"His name is Brandon Wright. I met him this afternoon. He's the sales rep for Allied Federated, and he's wonderful," she said with that same enthusiasm.

Oh, great, he's wonderful. Jack plastered on a polite smile. It wasn't the breaking news he'd wanted to hear.

"Get it, Jack? Mr. Wright as Mr. Right? I think it might be some kind of sign."

"It's a sign all right," Jack mumbled. "An evil omen."

"What? Did you say something?" she called out.

"I said"—he spoke louder—"all right—go, Meg!" He took a swig of ginger ale, settled on the sofa, and rubbed the back of his neck.

Jack had hoped Megan's dateless status would last until they went back to the Midwest. Who would have thought she'd meet someone only days before they were set to leave?

This was only a date, he told himself. One date. Megan was getting way ahead of herself thinking that this guy was Mr. Right, and Jack was overreacting.

"You're skeptical. I can understand that." Her voice echoed from the back room. "It's my life, and even I'm a little skeptical, but this might be it—the real thing."

"The *real thing*?" Jack whispered to himself in alarm.

This was terrible. Mr. Right had to be Mr. Wrong or at least Mr. Very Bad Timing. Only three days to go.

"You just met him this afternoon." Jack's voice went up an octave.

"There's something different about him. I can't put my finger on it, but I just get the feeling that we have a connection. You know? There's a certain connection two people make when things are . . . just right."

Yeah, he knew. It's the way he felt about Megan. Jack

clenched his fist. He'd like to make a connection—with Wright's face. No one messed with Jack's woman.

Except Megan didn't know she was his woman. She hadn't a clue.

A stocking-clad Megan stepped from the hallway wearing a figure-hugging number in black. At the sight of her, Jack choked; his outgoing "Wow!" collided with the incoming ginger ale.

"Are you okay?" Megan stepped closer, sounding concerned.

Sure, she cared that he might choke to death, but it didn't matter that she was about to break his heart.

"No—I mean, yes." Jack coughed and blinked his watering eyes. "I've never seen *that* dress before."

"I've had it in the back of the closet, saving it for something special." Sporting a smile, Megan did a three-sixty for his inspection. "What do you think?" She glanced at him over her shoulder, waiting to hear his opinion.

He set his ginger ale on the coffee table and circled Megan, taking a slow, good, very long look. What there was of the outfit was short and low and tight. So tight, she shouldn't have been able to breathe. Even her curves had curves.

"It's skimpy." The black material barely covered the parts that needed to be covered. "There isn't enough of it there to be called clothing."

"Skimpy? It goes all the way down to my knees. The sleeves go down to my elbows, and if the neck went any higher, it'd be a turtleneck. I'll admit, it's fitted in a few spots." She ran her hand along the curve of her waist and traced the outside of her thigh.

"Yeah, but those are the spots that could land you in jail for indecent exposure," he was quick to point out.

"I'm completely covered. Not even the slightest peek here or there."

Sure, that's what she wanted him to believe. But the truth of it was, he didn't want anyone else to peek at her *here and there.*

"Aren't you exaggerating a bit? This is a simple, classic black dress."

"You mean *little* black dress. Come on, Meg, cover up. Put on something decent."

" 'Something decent'? The only thing more decent than this is a muumuu. This is exactly what I want, something different. I need to shake up my act."

If Megan shook *anything,* he wanted it to be with him, not some sales rep. Jack's mind was running wild with ideas. He had to keep calm and trust that she knew what she was doing, that's all. And he could trust Megan. She had a good, smart head on those beautiful shoulders of hers.

"Look, let's not get wild here," he said. "We've got to be careful nowadays."

"You're right. Of course, you're right. I'm not planning to do anything rash—I just want to loosen up a bit."

Any looser *and there'd be a free peep show for the restaurant patrons.* He kept his cool and said, "I still think there's too much exposed flesh."

"I think you're being unreasonable, Jack." Megan flashed him a stern look. "I want to keep him interested, that's all."

"If he's not interested, he should have his head examined." Jack rubbed his forehead. It was no use. There was nothing he could say that would make her change clothes.

Megan stared at Jack's watch. "What time is it?" The minute hand was near the twelve and the hour hand between two numbers. It was hard to tell exactly what time it was. She grabbed Jack's wrist and turned his watch toward her, twisting his arm.

"Ouch, ouch, ouch!"

"It's almost seven. I've got to get moving." Megan dropped his wrist.

"Hey, that's my arm!" He grabbed his shoulder and rubbed.

"Sorry." She hurried to the bedroom for her shoes.

"So, Mr. Perfect isn't punctual?"

She grabbed hold of the doorjamb for balance and slipped her right shoe on. "I'm meeting him at Chez Louis—and, no, he isn't late." Megan sounded more than mildly impressed.

Jack's eyes widened when he mouthed, *Chez Louis*. It impressed him too. "You mean he hasn't the decency to pick you up?"

"It's meet him at the restaurant or put off dinner until after nine." Megan balanced on her right foot and stepped into her left shoe before stepping forward and striking a pose, letting him get the full effect.

Jack swallowed hard. "You don't think those shoes are overkill?"

"They go with the outfit. What time is it now?"

Jack checked his watch. "About five after seven."

"I've got to get going." She ran to the bedroom and came back with her purse. "Lock up for me, will you?"

"Sure. Have a good time," he called out to her just before she ran out the door. She looked beautiful and was going to an amazing restaurant—how could she not have a good time?

Jack just wished it was with him.

Megan made it to Chez Louis just in time to catch Brandon coming out the entrance to greet her. She couldn't wait for the evening to start. The whole way there she had been looking forward to the candlelight, crystal, and Champagne. And Brandon.

"You look fantastic" were his first words.

By the way his eyes were popping out of his head, she could have guessed that he liked her dress. She shrugged and replied, "Oh, this old thing?"

"And no place fancy to show you off. I'm so sorry. Our reservation got lost. We're on our own tonight."

On our own? Megan was dressed to impress, and she wanted to work her magic on Brandon. What was she supposed to do now?

"I promise, I'll make it up to you, okay?" Brandon looked truly sorry for the mix-up.

"It's all right, Brandon. Really," Megan reassured him, putting on a brave smile.

"I know this great little diner around the corner. They have the best burgers."

"Burgers." Megan met Brandon's wide smile with one of her own. "Sounds great." Wearing a gorgeous dress to eat hamburgers wasn't Megan's idea of a perfect date with Mr. Right, and she couldn't help feeling a little disappointed.

"Good." Brandon took her by the hand. "Let's get going. It'll only take a few minutes to walk."

Walk? Well, it was a nice evening. One might consider a stroll in the moonlight romantic. Yes, that's exactly what it was, she told herself.

Megan glanced down at her feet. She really wouldn't mind walking except her shoes were a bit tight around the toe, and the thin, decorative straps were already starting to rub. The high heels were strictly for looks, not function.

It didn't matter, she decided. Her sacrifice would be worth it, she was sure. And if she repeated that enough times, she might even believe it.

Jack could hardly believe it. Three days left before he and Megan would be alone. Three lousy, stinking days before he had a chance to prove himself to her, and *Mr. Right* had to crawl out from under his rock.

He sat with the remote control in one hand, a soda can in the other, and one leg dangling over an arm of the chair. He wasn't going to sit around his apartment and think about Megan. Megan out on the town with Mr. Right. Megan and *Mr. Right* in a fancy-schmancy, uptown restaurant.

This guy didn't even know her.

Jack knew her preference ran toward Chinese food, not fancy French cuisine. *It's only a date,* he kept telling himself. *One date.*

Jack dropped the remote control, tossed the can into the recycle bin, changed into his sweats, and headed for the gym.

He'd work it off with weights and lots of reps. But if this thing between him and Megan wasn't resolved soon, he'd end up looking like a bulked-up version of Mr. Universe.

He had just stepped out of the men's locker room when a breathy voice called to him, "Hello, Jack."

"Hi, Tina," Jack greeted the spandex-clad woman passing him on her way to the cardio room.

"You're here kind of late, aren't you?"

"I needed something to do." Jack draped his towel within arm's reach of the climbing-stair machine and concentrated on programming it for a bruising workout.

"Pent-up energy?" Tina puffed and eyed him up and down while pumping the pedals on the stationary bicycle two machines away from him.

"Something like that." Jack started climbing.

If only he could get the picture of Megan in that tight dress out of his mind—but he was fairly sure that wasn't going to happen.

Tina climbed off her bike and approached him. "Would you like me to give you a hand?" she said, enunciating every word between shallow breaths.

"Thanks, but I don't need a spotter. I won't be doing any free weights tonight."

She took a long look at him. "If you're sure you don't need me, I'll be going."

"Okay. See you around." Tina was breathing pretty hard, and Jack wondered if she'd overdone her workout.

After forty-five minutes, Jack headed for the leg-curl machine. He laid his towel on the padded rest and set the weight. He hooked his heels beneath the roller pad and pulled his lower legs toward his thighs, working his hamstrings.

After the first ten reps, a pretty blond strolled by and paused. "Hi, Jack. How you doing?"

Jack looked up. "Hi, Britney," he managed between controlled breaths. "Fine."

She trailed her fingers across her toned torso and batted her eyes. "Are you going to need someone to spot you?"

Jack pulled his heels up to his thighs for his last repetition. "No. Not today. Thanks." He extended his legs, lowering the weights.

"Sure. Anytime." Britney smiled. "Let me know if you change your mind."

"Will do."

"I guess I'll see you around, okay?"

"Okay." Jack untangled his legs from the machine and sat up. He wiped the sweat off his neck and forehead with his towel.

Another blond, on her way to the women's locker room, paused and looked at him. More than once. *That* was weird. She was staring at him as if he were a cold bottle of water.

Then it occurred to him. Okay, so he was a little slow.

It wasn't just Britney. It was all those women. Jack hadn't realized that so many women—young and attractive women—knew him. Nine months ago, he would have been glad they noticed him. He might even have asked them out. But not anymore.

He wasn't interested in any of them. Not now. The only woman Jack wanted was Megan.

So why hadn't he said anything to her about the way he felt? Or done anything about it? Why was he putting it off?

Because Jack didn't want to risk losing what he had with her—their friendship.

Megan was just too important to him.

Chapter Four

Megan swung into her side of the diner booth and faced Brandon. She didn't even look down at her feet. Her shoes—and her toes—were likely beyond repair.

The fancy footwear might have lasted through dozens of trips to the ladies' room and back on plush carpeting, even on hardwood flooring or marble, but the three-block hike on concrete had taken its toll on the obscenely expensive, delicately built sling-backs. So much for saving them for a special occasion.

Every pebble larger than a grain of sand she stepped on threatened, if not poked through, the paper-thin soles. Both heels had begun wobbling halfway through the journey, and she nearly lost her left heel altogether when she took the stairs into the diner. Megan would be lucky if her feet weren't covered in blisters, but she wasn't complaining.

If Brandon turned out to be the man of her dreams, the comfort of her feet would be a small price to pay. She could tell that Brandon had felt bad about the reservation mix-up.

It didn't matter where they ate; this was still a special

occasion—their first date. All that mattered was that she was with him and that all he cared about was her. That was a good sign. It hadn't been the same with her other boyfriends. The only other person who treated her that way—Megan first—was Jack.

Megan picked up her menu and noticed that Brandon hadn't touched his. He must come here often. "Do you know what you're having?"

"The Mondo burger and a chocolate shake."

"Sounds good. Do you want to share some fries?"

"You're on." He winked at her.

The waitress—Laura, according to her badge— stopped at their table. Was it Megan's imagination, or did Laura do a double take?

Yes, Megan could admit, she was overdressed. There was nothing she could do about it; she'd been destined for Chez Louis, not a burger shack.

"Are you ready to order?" Laura glanced at each of them in turn.

"We'll have two Mondo burgers, an order of fries, and two chocolate shakes." Brandon held up the menus, returning them.

Laura jotted down the order, collected the menus, and stepped away.

"I'm really sorry about tonight, Megan," he said for the fiftieth time, placing his hands over hers on the Formica table. "I must be really making an impression, bringing you to a diner for our first date." He glanced around, sounding just as unhappy at their last-minute change in venue. "I'll make it up to you." His warm, wide smile reassured her that he meant every word.

"There's nothing to make up for."

"I can't believe my rotten luck." He closed his eyes and shook his head slowly in amazement. "I finally meet someone I want to spend some time with, and the next thing I know, my boss sends me out of town."

"Out of town?" *No, not now.* Not when they had just found each other.

"It's business. I'm leaving tomorrow."

"Tomorrow?" This was horrible.

"I'll be back on Thursday," he continued.

Thursday? She was going to Iowa with Jack on Thursday. "*I'll* be out of town. But we're coming back on Sunday." What she needed to do was to stay home and work on this budding relationship with Brandon.

"*We?*"

"Ah, yes." This was tough part, but Megan wasn't going to lie. That would be a horrible way to start off with a guy. "I'm going to a wedding with my friend Jack."

"Jack? Is this someone else you're seeing?"

"No. No, it's not like that at all. Jack's just a friend, really." She chuckled nervously. "I've known him for years, since high school." Megan could tell right off that Brandon wasn't comfortable with the notion of Jack.

But Megan wasn't going to put up with any jealousy—a lesson she'd learned from her ex-boyfriend Greg.

"Really, Brandon"—she smiled reassuringly—"there's nothing going on between Jack and me."

Brandon returned her smile; she must have put him at ease. "How about lunch when you get back on Monday?"

Monday was good. "Perfect."

"Shall we try Chez Louis again?" he whispered in a tone that tempted her to lose her heart to him.

Brandon really did want to make it up to her, and she was slipping, ready to make the dive. "You know, I think that place is highly overrated. Why don't we try the Chinese restaurant around the corner?"

"Taste of Hong Kong?"

"That's the one. It's one of my favorites. I love Chinese food."

Brandon laughed. "You know, Megan, I really *do* like you." He squeezed her hand. "I hope you don't feel like I'm rushing things between us. It's just that . . . I feel we really could have something special."

So Megan wasn't the only one who felt it.

The chocolate shakes came first. They were in tall, frosted glasses with a dollop of whipped cream. The waitress brought the hamburgers and a single order of fries, piled so high, they threatened to slide off the plate.

Megan cleared a space in front of her for the burger. "These are big burgers."

"They don't call them Mondo for nothing." Brandon took the ketchup and Megan the mustard.

She opened the top and squeezed. Nothing. She could never get these things to work. Shaking the bottle, she tried again, squeezing harder.

A stream of yellow shot out of the mustard container and hit Brandon's chest. It happened so fast—

"I'm so sorry!" Megan couldn't help the instantaneous flashback of her ex-boyfriend Daniel of clothes-make-the-man fame. He never could have laughed off his shirt's being soiled. He swore that even a water drop left a mark. Then again, Daniel's shirts probably cost more than ten burgers and milkshakes and fries put together.

Brandon merely chuckled at the mishap. Megan couldn't believe it; he just laughed.

"I wish you could have seen the look on your face," he managed through his chuckles.

"I'm *really* sorry." Megan tried to keep from cracking up and handed him a wad of paper napkins. "I've ruined your shirt."

Brandon reached for the napkins but took hold of her hands instead and gazed into her eyes. "Maybe . . . but you gave me a good chuckle."

She couldn't stop a sigh from escaping. He was a prince—that much was for sure. The way things were shaping up, she couldn't stop hoping that she had finally found the man she'd been looking for.

It was about time. She'd been looking hard enough.

After dinner Brandon followed her back to her apartment. He still hadn't lost his luster. Pulling the keys out of her purse, Megan couldn't help but feel a little nervous as she unlocked her door.

Do I or don't I invite him in? Kiss him good-night?

She wanted to, but the thought was a little unsettling. It had only been one date—a fantastic, memorable one, but still, only one.

"Is that where *he* lives?" Brandon jerked his thumb at the door next to hers.

"No. We already passed his place. He lives down that way, across the hall." Her hands trembled, but not enough to make unlocking the door a problem.

"Do you think I should have a word with him?" Brandon's territorial message held a light tone; of course he was only joking.

Megan opened the door and faced Brandon. "I don't think you need to."

How could she think of Jack when she had this big hunk of a guy, totally interested, right in front of her?

Brandon leaned casually against the doorjamb as if he had all the time in the world to wait and crossed his legs at the ankle. As if he was expecting something. "Is Jack blind?"

"Blind?"

"You expect me to believe he's only your *friend*?"

"I'm just not his type." Feeling a bit embarrassed, she gave a half shrug and small smile. The last thing she wanted was for Jack to step outside and catch her in the hallway with Brandon. But she still wasn't about to invite Brandon in.

Guilt was what she felt. Just one notch under *cheating-on-Jack*. But it wasn't possible for her to cheat on Jack.

"I don't know if I can wait until next week to see you again." Brandon brushed a finger along her cheek.

Megan fought the shiver that went through her. It felt odd. Not odd good, odd bad.

All wrong.

"What do you think about my coming in for a while?" he tempted her in an oh-so-dreamy tone filled with promises.

"I don't think so," she said, knowing this was going to majorly disappoint Leslie.

"Okay," he conceded. "How about a good-night kiss?"

She stared at Brandon, then glanced down the hall toward Jack's, hoping that he wouldn't come out. That was silly. As if he would care.

Her feet hurt.

They were a constant reminder of spending the last evening with Brandon. How she managed to make it through a day's work, she'd never know.

Megan wheeled around the office on her chair a lot, and Leslie worked as her personal gofer all day long. That was, between demanding a minute-by-minute, very detailed report of her last night's date.

Leslie wanted to know everything. *Everything.* But to Leslie's disappointment and Megan's embarrassment, there wasn't a whole lot to tell. The evening had ended with a peck on her cheek.

Megan couldn't bring Leslie home with her, no matter how much she'd wanted or needed to, and it was too bad. After starting her first load of wash, Megan could barely make it up the stairs from the laundry room. With the second load in hand, she stood at the top of the stairs and thought about her clothes in the washing machine chugging away three floors below. They might as well have been in Antarctica.

She shifted her weight and winced. Her poor feet. Gripping the handrail, Megan braced herself and took the first excruciating step.

I don't know if I can make it.

No, she couldn't go any farther. What if she got stuck midway on the stairs? How would she get back up? She glanced over her shoulder at her apartment door. She wasn't even sure she could make it back home.

What about the clothes already downstairs in the washer? By tomorrow morning they'd be piled on top of the worktable in a wet, wrinkled, moldy mess. She was sure no one would steal them. Well, she was pretty sure.

"Megan, are you all right?"

A door closed behind her, and Jack took the laundry basket, which made Megan feel about two tons lighter. She used both hands to pull herself up to the landing.

"You're limping!" He set her laundry basket down in the hallway and wrapped a supporting arm around her. "What's wrong?"

"Oh, Jack. My feet hurt so bad." She laid her arm across his shoulders and leaned against him.

"Let's get you inside." He scooped her into his arms.

Megan thought men only did that in movies, but Jack proved her wrong.

"How did you hurt your feet?" Jack shifted his arms, making sure she was comfortable. He held her as if he could have stood there forever.

"Those shoes I wore last night."

"Too many trips to the ladies' room?"

"Good one, funny guy. I didn't think I'd be trekking down to Taylor and Main Street."

"I thought you were having dinner at Chez Louis?"

"We ended up eating at the diner." That sounded awful—tacky, somehow. She then added, "You know, the cozy one next door to the First United Bank?"

Jack smiled. "What happened to Chez Louis?" He started down the hall to her apartment.

"There was a mix-up. They lost our reservation." With her arms around Jack's neck, Megan thought she could get used to being this close to him. He felt firm, solid, comfortable. *Rats.* In two or three more steps he'd be at her place; then he'd put her down.

"*Lost* your reservation?" Jack pushed her apartment door open, stepped inside with an armful of Megan, and headed for the sofa.

"It happens," she said in Brandon's defense. "This isn't the first time it's happened to me."

"I believe you." Jack stepped in and laid her on the sofa. Gently.

"Wait a minute," she called after him. "I still have

clothes in the washer. I can't make it down there *again.*" She sounded whiny, even to herself.

"That's all right. You just sit," he told her in a tone that said he'd take care of everything.

"You're so wonderful, Jack. Here." Megan dug some quarters out of her front pocket and dropped them into his hand. "My wash is in—"

"Number seven," he said with her, and he smiled. "Stay put until I get back."

Would Brandon have done this for her? *Of course he would,* she reassured herself. *He would.* "Don't worry. I'm not going anywhere. Thanks, Jack. You're a life-saver."

Jack pulled the door closed behind him. He snagged her laundry basket on his way down the stairs and said to himself, "Yeah, I always score big for being a nice guy."

Down in the laundry room, Jack pulled Megan's wash out of washer number seven and dropped it into dryer number three. That's the way Megan would have done it.

First out were a couple pairs of slacks and some dark sweats. A couple shirts followed. He shook them out before putting them into number three.

"I wore this knock-'em-dead dress just for you, Brandon," he said in a sweet, high-pitched, female voice, mimicking Megan.

One by one, Jack tossed dark-colored cotton socks into the dryer.

"Okay. Let's go to the dingy burger joint," he answered himself in the exaggerated baritone he imagined for Brandon.

He tossed in a dryer sheet, closed the door, pushed the money into the machine, and started the tumble cycle. Back at the washing machine, Jack reset the knob from colors to whites and pushed the quarters home.

The washer lurched into motion, pouring water into the tub. He measured in the detergent and tried not to look at her whites as he put them in.

Whites could be dangerous. They were little cotton nothings, tiny tees, wispy women things that he didn't want to think about. *None of his business*—not unlike Megan's love life.

Jack dropped three pairs of white cotton socks in like payloads from a bomber flying overhead, making the whistling sound of their descent into the washer water.

He didn't know how or why, but this time was different. This *Brandon* made Jack nervous. Megan had never raved about a guy this way before.

No one was that cool or that great.

There were only two more days until he'd be alone with Megan.

Closing the washer lid with care, Jack closed his eyes. Then it finally dawned on him. He'd lost his chance with her.

Chapter Five

"Honey, I'm home!" Jack sounded all happy. "Colors in the dryer—done! Whites in the wash—done! Jack's back, and he's ready, willing, and able."

Megan pushed herself upright, peering over the back of the sofa. "What?" He held a small blue plastic tub in one hand and a box of Epsom salt in the other, and he headed for the kitchen sink. "What are you doing?"

He ran the water and measured out the salts with one hand. "We're leaving for Iowa the day after tomorrow, remember? I can't have you gimping around injured. I've got to have you up and raring to go. You need to put your feet into my hands. Trust me, will you?"

"Oh, yeah. Your sister's wedding." She hadn't forgotten, just slid the occasion onto the back burner. Megan couldn't help it if her feet had taken over her life—they hurt.

Jack pushed the coffee table to one side, set the plastic tub near Megan's feet, pulled off her socks, and guided her feet toward the water. "Soak your tootsies in here, and tell me all about your big night."

"Come on, I don't want to put my feet in there." She

45

resisted. "This is—" *Ridiculous,* is what she wanted to say, but Megan could feel herself melting from the ankles down, and she sank deeper into the cushions. "This feels pretty good."

"Yes, it does." Jack patted her knee before rounding the sofa and taking his place behind her, ready for the next treatment. "I must have been a healer in a prior life. Just call me Jack-of-the-Magic-Hands." He straightened his arms, flexing his fingers in front of her before setting to work.

The massage hurt a little at first. Megan hadn't realized how tense the muscles in her shoulders were.

"It's not only your feet that are sore, you know. You hold the pain throughout your body." Rubbing gently at first, he moved from her shoulders to the base of her neck.

"I didn't know that," she whispered. Those were the last words spoken for . . . she didn't know how long. Soon she couldn't move her mouth at all; she couldn't form a single word. Megan's neck, head, and body were feeling heavier by the minute, so relaxed.

Had five minutes gone by, or had it been fifteen? She might have even fallen asleep. She'd felt so tired, and Jack's fingers seemingly infused her with youth. She went from tired and sore to completely relaxed, then totally energized.

"Tell me all about your date last night. Did you behave yourself? And, more important, did Brandon behave himself?"

"Of course he did. And I did too."

"So . . . did you have a good time? Is he . . . *Mr. Right*?"

Jack's ministrations made Megan sigh before she spoke. "It was a perfect first date."

"Barring the shoes, that is," Jack added.

"All except for the shoes," Megan agreed. "He was a perfect gentleman." Which mattered to her. She was tired of the kind of guy who didn't even hint at having any manners. This time she had found a nice guy. Someone like Jack. "Did I tell you that he called me today?"

"No, you didn't. Do tell—I'm all ears."

"He felt so bad about the mix-up at the restaurant, but he promised me we'd go back."

"Did he?"

"I told him we don't ever have to go back. It doesn't matter to me."

"And I'll bet he didn't argue."

"He really wants to take me to some nice places and spend some quality time together. But you know me—I don't need fancy restaurants or expensive desserts. Give me a slice of pot roast and a bowl of ice cream, and I'm happy."

"Rocky Road, right?" Jack sat on the floor next to the plastic tub and held out a towel to dry her feet.

"I love the little marshmallows."

Jack nudged her to move over to give him some room. Megan scooted toward one end of the sofa, and he sat on the other with her feet resting in his lap.

"Strawberry is another favorite." He kneaded the

bottoms of her feet, making them ache but feel oh-so-good all at the same time.

"Oh, that's tasty too." He knew exactly what she liked. What was he doing? His warm hands were touching, rubbing, the tender parts of her feet.

"And there's mocha chip," he added. He knew her so well. "And chocolate chocolate chip."

"Mmmm . . . those little chocolate chunks." Every muscle in Megan's body was melting along with her voice. She was the melt-ee and Jack was the melt-er. "Nothing wrong with liking ice cream."

"Isn't it one of the major food groups?" Jack set her foot on his chest and rubbed the outside of her leg, soothing the muscles. "I prefer—"

"The oowie-gooey caramel kind." There was nothing better than chocolate *and* caramel.

"Hey, we all have our weaknesses."

Oh, yes we do. Some people could indulge, and some couldn't. Megan knew on which side of the weakness fence she fell. Her weakness was Jack.

"That hurts so good." She groaned, not from pain but from relief. And it went on and on as he rubbed and rubbed. Megan hovered between torment and pleasure.

There was a knock at the door.

Well, that broke the mood.

Megan tensed and sat straight up. "I wonder who that could be," she said, hoarse and breathless. Without considering her once-sore feet, she stood and headed for the door.

Jack hefted the discarded footbath to the bathroom.

"Brandon, what are you doing here?" Megan's voice held more nervous apprehension than delight at the man's unexpected appearance.

Brandon?

"I thought you were going out of town."

Jack set the rubber tub on the bathroom counter before tiptoeing back down the hall and peeking around the corner to get a look at his competition.

"I'm on my way to the airport now. I had to see you before I left."

Looking past Megan, all Jack could see of Brandon was an armful of flowers and a smarmy smile. Okay, so he might possibly be attractive to women if they went for the fair-haired, handsome, hunky type.

"These are for you." Brandon held out the bouquet of mixed flowers.

Megan took the flowers and pecked Brandon on the cheek.

That was a sorriest excuse for a kiss Jack ever saw. It was an obligatory kiss on her part. It the worst kind of a kiss for a man to get.

Brandon had surprised her. It was a pathetic maneuver.

The man wrapped his arms around Megan and tried to hold her close. There was a definite pushing back on Megan's part, and with a few small steps she put some distance between them.

She held the bouquet to her nose, effectively creating a barrier between them. "These smell great. This is really sweet of you." Jack could hear the forced smile in her voice. "I don't know what to say."

"Say that you'll make Monday a memorable day. Give me something to look forward to," the sleazy rat crooned.

The guy was hiding something, and Jack knew it. That guy was giving off weird vibes. Nobody was that perfect. Nobody.

"Okay," Megan answered quickly, hesitantly, and nervously. Jack had also noticed that she hadn't bothered to ask her new beau inside.

That told Jack everything he needed to know.

"See you on Monday." Brandon's smooch on her cheek would have been audible from Jack's own apartment.

Jack pulled back from the corner and felt a smile spread across his face. He didn't know Brandon, but he knew Megan. Jack could tell that she wasn't as enchanted with her new suitor as she'd led him to believe.

And tomorrow he'd be going away for the weekend with her. He had to win her heart before Brandon pried himself into Megan's life.

He'd been wrong. Now Jack knew he still had a chance with Megan.

After work, Jack knocked on the door of Megan's apartment and yelled, "It's me!"

"Come on in," she called out from her bedroom.

Jack stepped inside with his two small brown paper bags and headed for the fridge. He cradled the bags in one arm and used his free hand to unbutton and cuff one sleeve of his white dress shirt.

"I'll be out in just a minute."

Jack cuffed his other sleeve on his way to the kitchen and pulled open the fridge door, helping himself to a can of ginger ale.

Megan stepped out from her bedroom and glanced at him, then at the door.

"Cute pink top." He leaned against the counter and took a drink of ginger ale.

"It didn't used to be pink."

"It didn't?" he asked, wide-eyed. "What happened?"

"Remember when you did the wash the other day?"

Jack's face warmed. *Oh, no. He didn't.*

"I'm sorry, Meg."

"Don't worry about it. You were nice enough to do my laundry for me, so I'm not going to complain. Besides, I think I like this color."

It didn't hurt that she was an absolute doll. Megan would look good in anything.

"What's in here?" She pulled one of the paper bags Jack had brought in and peered inside.

"Dinner. Chinese chicken salad, rice, and the General's chicken. I figured we'd be low on supplies."

"You mean *food*?"

"It's a basic necessity."

She laughed and pulled the second bag toward her. "And what's in here? You did *not* buy more ice cream.

We've got tons. We could open our own store." She opened a drawer and pulled out the scooper.

"It never goes bad. Ice cream doesn't turn into a science experiment."

"Ice cream doesn't last long enough around here to go bad."

That much was true.

Jack reached into the cupboard for two bowls. "It's mint chocolate chip. I thought we'd be adventurous tonight before we fly off into the wild blue yonder!"

They made it to the airport, through security, to the gate, and down the Jetway in record time. This was Jack's big chance with Megan. Alone on the plane with her for the entire five-hour flight. He couldn't ask for more.

If things went well between them, they'd be holding hands and cuddling all the way home. This was uncharted, scary territory, but he couldn't wait for it to finally happen.

Megan sat in the window seat. Jack took the aisle and stowed his backpack under the seat in front of him before fastening his seat belt. He glanced over at her.

Jack wanted his family to get to know her, and he wanted Megan to meet them. For now, he had to keep his own feelings under wraps. He just had to play it safe, cool—for the time being.

Jack turned to her. "Would you like to play cards?"

"Cards? I'd love to. I love playing cards."

"Really?" He pulled a new deck of playing cards from his carry-on. "I never knew that."

"So . . ." She lowered a arm between them. "There are *some* things you don't know about me."

"You don't know everything about me, either." Opening the pack, Jack shuffled the new cards and returned her smile. "What are we playing?"

"Gin?"

He nodded and dealt the cards, glancing up at her periodically. He set the deck between them and picked up his cards. Megan studied her hand.

She sure was adorable. How could someone look so *cute* playing cards?

Jack hoped his timing was right. He was going to do his best to make Megan forget all about Mr. Wright.

"Dad!" Jack called out to his father, who was waiting outside the security gate at the Des Moines airport.

"Hey, boy!" Jack's dad gave him a great bear hug. "Good to see you, son."

The men broke apart, and Jack motioned for Megan to come forward. "Megan, this is my dad, Robert."

Robert held Megan at arm's length and gave her the once-over. "So you're Jack's little lady."

Jack flashed her an apologetic smile.

"Nice to meet you, Mr. Meredith." She held the strap of her travel bag on her shoulder and reached out to shake his hand.

"It's Robert, please. Here, let me take that for you." He lifted Megan's bag onto his shoulder.

"Thanks."

Robert winked, smiled wide, handed her shoulder tote to Jack, and happily escorted her to the baggage-claim area. Megan stood off to one side with their carry-on bags while Jack and his father went to the carousel to retrieve the checked items.

Jack had a lot of his father in him. They looked alike—tall, slender build, and they even walked the same way.

"Okay, we're ready to go," Jack announced, lugging his bag and both of her checked pieces.

Robert Meredith led the way out of the terminal to his car. "Gotta lot of chores waiting for you back home."

Chores? Megan glanced to Jack, hoping for some insight. Weren't they here for a wedding?

"There's plenty, let me tell you," his dad went on.

Jack leaned toward Megan and whispered, "Dad's always got something lined up for me when I come home."

"Jeff, Andy, and Roy are getting a head start as we speak, but there'll be more than enough work to go around." Robert stopped behind a giant bronze sedan and popped the trunk open.

"Andy and Roy are Jeff's brothers," Jack told her.

Megan already knew that Jeff Latimer was marrying Jack's sister Shelley. Within the next forty-eight hours, Megan figured she'd know everyone's names on both sides of the family.

The luggage went into the trunk. Jack rode shotgun,

and Megan sat in the backseat. They drove for about two hours, first on the freeway and then an hour on back roads.

Jack and his dad spent the time catching up, and Megan sat quietly. Just as she was thinking that they had to be getting close, the Buick turned left, pulling onto gravel—a driveway. An older, two-story white farmhouse with dark green trim came into view. They passed a small weathered silo and a slightly leaning barn with attached paddock that looked as if it had been deserted for quite a while.

Mr. Meredith parked in front of the house. Megan stepped out of the car and took a deep breath of clear, clean, country air. The warm smell of hay and various earthy, animal aromas reminded her of her own home state of Nebraska. The country was the same no matter what the midwestern state—beautiful.

Across from the house was a huge, open-sided white tent. For the wedding reception, Megan assumed. She followed Robert and Jack up solid wooden steps, across a wide porch, and into the house.

Mr. Meredith stepped inside first. "Mother, we're home."

Footsteps sounded from the right. Jack stopped just inside the door. Megan followed him into a high-ceilinged parlor.

A tall woman with shoulder-length dark hair came in, wiping her hands on her apron. "Oh, honey, I'm glad you're home. It's so good to see you."

Jack took his mother into his arms. She kissed his

cheek, wrapped her arms around Jack's waist, and held him tightly for a hug.

Jack stepped back and held out a hand to Megan. "Mom, I want you to meet Megan." She stepped forward. "This is my mother, Ellen."

"It's nice to meet you, dear." There was a lot of Ellen Meredith in Jack too, around the eyes and in the warm, welcoming grin that lifted the corners of her mouth. "I'm glad Jack's finally met a girl he likes enough to bring home."

Jack's never brought anyone home to meet his family—ever? Megan hoped his family wasn't expecting too much from her.

"I hope you three are hungry." Ellen slipped her arm around Robert. "I've planned a big supper."

"Are you kidding?" Jack took hold of Megan's hand and started to lead her toward the kitchen. "I'm always hungry."

"You can say that again," Megan agreed.

"Hey!" Jack seemed to take exception.

"Hold on. Why don't you take your things upstairs and get settled first?" Ellen Meredith said to Jack. "Don't take too long. You need to go into town before dinner to have your tux fitted. Ed Friese is keeping his store open after hours for you." She turned to her husband. "Dad, why don't you drive Jack and Megan into town?"

"All right, Mother," Robert answered.

"I know where his shop is." Jack tried to shake his

dad off. If this was the way the weekend went, he'd never have any time alone with Megan.

"I'm sorry, but we're short on space." Ellen gestured to the variety of gifts in silver and white wrapping paper stacked high in several corners. Sprays of tulle sprouting out the tops of other open boxes were probably some kind of wedding favors.

"Pamela and Steve are in her old room, and their girls will be in sleeping bags on the floor," Ellen said over her shoulder. She stopped at the foot of the stairs. "The guest room and your old room are empty, but I'm not sure where you two will be sleeping. It depends on who shows up tonight. For now, why don't you put your things in your old room?"

"I'll pop the trunk for you, son." *Thanks, Dad.* That was a subtle get-your-own-luggage hint.

Megan laid a hand on Jack's arm. "You stay in here with your mom. I'll help your dad with the luggage," she said, and she headed out the front door.

Good thinking, Meg. There'd be no way Dad would let Megan lug all the bags into the house by herself.

Chapter Six

The town, it turned out, was a half hour away. It was fifteen minutes to the residential areas, then fifteen more to the store. Robert pulled up to a place called Ed's Tailoring.

Megan followed Jack and Robert toward the store. She looked down the street at the signs, the shops, and the shopkeepers who were busy locking up for the night. She'd forgotten how it was out here.

It was just after five in the afternoon, but these were farm towns, and they kept country hours. Shops were open early and closed early. Most of the citizens woke at sunrise and were ready for bed by sunset.

"Thanks for staying open late, Mr. Friese," Jack said, going into the store. He held the glass door open for Megan and his dad.

"No, problem, Jack. How you doing?" Ed shook Jack's hand.

"I'm just fine. Thanks for asking. Is this my tux?" Jack pointed to a light gray tux on a hanger behind Ed Friese.

"Ah, yeah." Ed snagged the hanger and handed it to Jack. "You know where to change."

Jack took the suit and headed toward the back where Ed had pointed.

"Who's this lovely lady?"

"This is Megan Donnelly. She's a friend of Jack's." Robert motioned to her.

"Is this how they grow 'em in California?" Ed asked.

"No." Megan smiled. "I'm from Nebraska. I just live in California."

"Should have known you'd be a midwestern gal. They don't grow 'em this pretty out west."

Jack came back. He looked like a boy wearing his dad's suit. The coat sleeves were long, the waist looked a little baggy, and the pants hung loose around his legs.

"Step on up over here." Ed indicated that he wanted Jack to stand in front of the mirror. "My, you've grown."

"Apparently not enough to fill this out," Jack replied.

"It's nothing we can't fix." Ed eyed the fit of Jack's trousers, smoothed the fabric across his shoulders, and pulled the back of the jacket taut. "You have to get the fit right across the shoulders—that's the important part." Ed made a couple of vertical marks next to the seams below Jack's arms with a piece of chalk.

Another mark at each cuff. "How do those trousers feel around the waist?"

"A little baggy, but nothing a belt can't take care of."

More marks down the legs. "The hem is fine. Okay,

I guess that's it. You can go ahead and change." Ed picked up the invoice and made some notes. "I can have this ready for pickup tomorrow afternoon about one—how's that?"

"Sounds good, Ed." Jack headed back to the changing room.

"You and the Latimer boys are all set, right?" He was asking about the groom, Jeff, and his brothers Andy and Roy, the groomsmen.

Robert nodded.

"And what about Billy?" Ed asked. Billy was Jack's nephew, his sister's Pamela's son.

"I'm not sure. Ellen would know."

The phone rang.

"Excuse me." Ed held up his index finger, punctuating the ensuing silence, then answered the phone. "Hello, Ed's Tailoring." He paused and glanced over at Robert. "Howdy, Ellen. Yeah, he's here. Your wife wants a word with you."

Robert took the receiver. "Hello. Yeah. Okay. We can do that—no problem."

"Ask about Billy," Ed whispered.

"Oh, right. Honey, what are we doing with Billy's tux? Uh-huh. Okay. I'll tell him. All right, I'll see you in a bit. Bye." Robert hung up the phone. "We'll be bringing him in first thing tomorrow."

"Sounds good."

Jack returned and handed his tux to Ed.

"Let's get going," Robert said. "And Mom says Aunty Max just got there."

"Aunty Max." Jack smiled, a flash of warm remembrance sparking in his eyes. "Meg, you're going to love my Aunty Max."

Maxine Pringle was Robert's aunt and Jack's great-aunt but was fondly known to all in the family as Aunty Max. She greeted Robert and Jack with a hug and a kiss.

"Oh, well, look at you." Aunty Max held Jack at arm's distance. "Handsome as ever." Then she turned toward Megan. "And who is this?"

Jack made the introductions.

Maxine's soft, white, curly hair resembled cotton balls covering her head, giving her the quintessential kindly-little-old-lady look.

"Oh, Jack, she's beautiful." Aunty Max's soft, round, wrinkled face lit up with a smile before she pulled Megan toward her and gave her a squeeze.

"Nice to meet you too, Mrs. Pringle." Megan shot Jack a sheepish smile. No one, especially a stranger, had ever greeted her in such a warm, welcoming manner.

"No, no, no. You have to call me Aunty Max. Everyone does."

"They do," Jack agreed. "You should too."

"Now you three sit down. I'll heat your supper up right now. Everyone's already eaten and gone back to work." Ellen Meredith flipped on the stove before stepping to the cabinet to grab some plates. "The women are in the parlor, making the wreaths, and the men are in the tent, hanging the lights."

"Let me give you a hand, Ellen." Aunty Max pushed past Robert and Jack to take the plates. "I'll take care of the drinks. Robert? Jack? What'll you be having?"

"Ginger ale," Jack and Robert chorused. They sat next to each other at the table.

"Megan, will you get some glasses out of the cabinet there?"

Megan opened the cabinet door and pulled out three glasses, handing them one by one to Aunty Max.

"Do you want some pop too, dear?" Aunty Max dropped ice cubes into a glass and set it on the counter.

Before Megan could answer, a woman's giggling drifted into the room. A moment later Jeff Latimer, the prospective groom, stepped in, moving backward through the kitchen, dragging Shelley Meredith in with him.

"Are you sure you can manage on your own?" Jeff gazed lovingly into Shelley's eyes and took another step toward the door, apparently oblivious to the crowd standing around them.

"I think you're the most talented man on earth, but I don't think you can style a flower wreath, no matter how hard you try." Shelley kissed his cheek. "You just don't want to climb up on the ladder and finish hanging those lights."

"I'd much rather spend time with you," he countered.

"You're such a bad liar—now get out there so I can get back to work."

Jeff gave Shelley a long, lingering kiss before he left, proving he was not lying about wanting to spend time with her. The kiss spiked the kitchen temperature about ten degrees.

"Food's warmed up," Ellen announced.

"And the ice is melted." Aunty Max emptied the glass into the sink.

They finished eating nearly a half hour later, and Robert Meredith pushed away from the table. "All right, I guess I'll head out to the tent. I'll see if I can offer a helping hand."

"They should be about finished hanging those lights, don't you think?" Ellen picked up his dirty dishes and brought them to the sink.

"Then I've timed it right, haven't I?" Robert stood and headed for the back door, making it out just before the commotion started.

"Uncle Jack!" a trio of young girls sang.

"Oh, no. They're coming!" Jack leaped out of his seat and "hid" behind Megan's chair.

A moment later *they* came bustling into the kitchen. Three blond-haired girls, small, smaller, and smallest in their flannel pajamas. Pamela's girls, Brittney, Sarah, and Jennifer.

"Oh, no, it's a munchkin invasion!" Jack shrieked in

mock horror. "Megan, save me!" He grabbed her shoulders from behind. "Don't let them get me! Don't let them get me!"

Megan laughed. "Sorry, Jack." She pried his fingers off her. "Every man for himself."

The girls took hold of their uncle and dragged him toward the parlor. "Come on, Uncle Jack," they chorused. "We want to show you! We want you to see how beautiful we are!"

"Good-bye, Megan. Good-bye, Mom. Good-bye, Aunty Max," Jack uttered melodramatically before disappearing through the door to the parlor.

"You really should go out there and be with the kids, Megan," Ellen urged, picking up the empty plates from the table. "Go on, Max, and I'll finish cleaning up."

Megan nodded, brought her plate to the sink, and followed them out the door. All three girls lined up in angelic fashion, modeling their silk flowered wreaths.

Each girl wore a halo of small-petaled, white silk flowers with several thin satin ribbons trailing down their backs.

"They're all going to make lovely flower girls," Megan said.

"I'm not a flower girl. I'm a junior bridesmaid," Brittney, the oldest, corrected. "My ribbons are *lavender*!" She turned her head to show Megan.

"And so they are," Megan admitted, noticing the minor color variation.

"Look, Mom, there's Uncle Jack!" A little boy came

flying down the stairs, trailing the scent of freshly washed youth. "He's here! He's here!"

"I see him, Billy." She must have been Pamela, Jack's elder sister.

"Hey, buddy!" Jack held out his arms for his nephew. "Come here, you little rascal. What are you up to?"

"We went to Burger Hut and everything today," Billy gushed.

"You did? Wow!" Jack returned with equal enthusiasm.

Going to a burger joint wasn't such a big deal in California, but, come to think of it, Megan hadn't seen a Burger Hut anywhere within Caldwell's city limits.

"I got a kid's meal. Look what toy I got—Cubby!" Billy held up a plastic movie character Megan didn't recognize.

"All right," Pamela broke in. "I think it's time for bed."

"But, Mom." Brittney whined, "we're not finished yet. We still have to—"

"Are we going to go fishing tomorrow?" Billy asked, bouncing from Jack's lap.

"We're gonna be busy with chores tomorrow, and your Aunt Shelley will be getting married the day after that."

"Oh," Billy groaned in disappointment.

"Don't worry. We boys will have a good time. You'll see."

"It's late. How about if you get right to bed? You can help the men in the morning," Pamela suggested.

"Cool!" Apparently whatever Uncle Jack liked, Billy liked too.

"We have work to do tomorrow, and everyone has to get up early," Jack told them.

"You're no fun, Uncle Jack," Jennifer, the youngest, protested.

"That's not what I hear," Jack sang, sporting an enormous smile, glancing at the one standing in the middle. Megan could see how much he enjoyed teasing his nieces.

"Did you tell him?" Sarah, the middle girl, demanded.

"I didn't tell him you liked him."

"I never said that," Sarah growled. "You're such a tattletale, Jennifer!"

And it wasn't so surprising that they found him irresistible.

"Girls, girls, it's okay," Jack interrupted. "You're supposed to like me—I'm your uncle." He kissed Jennifer on the forehead and took off her wreath. "Night-night, Jenn. See you in the morning."

"Night, Uncle Jack." Jennifer took her mother's hand and headed toward the stairs.

"I'm going to be the first one in bed!" Billy called out, and he made a mad dash for the stairs.

"See you in the morning, Billy." Jack pulled Brittney toward him by one arm, removed her wreath, and planted a kiss on her forehead. "Night, Brittney."

"Good night, Uncle Jack." She gave him a big hug and left.

Sarah had already removed her wreath and handed it to Jack. "Good night, Uncle Jack."

Jack swept her off her feet and into his arms. "Don't worry, Sarah." He rubbed noses with her. "I like you too." He spun her around in circles, and she gave a high-pitched squeal. Stopping at the door, he set her down in the hall near the staircase.

"Oh, I'm dizzy." Sarah stretched out her arms for balance.

"Come on, honey. I'll help you up." Pamela steadied her and led her up the stairs.

Shelley leveled a glare at Jack. "You heartbreaker, you."

"Can I help that I'm irresistible to the opposite sex?" He shrugged.

"Oh, please." Shelley rolled her eyes.

Ellen and Aunty Max came in from the kitchen.

"Where are the kids?" Ellen asked.

"Pamela's putting them to bed," Shelley replied. "She'll be back in a couple of minutes."

"Pamela and Steve will be staying in the guest room," Ellen told them. "Maxine and Megan will be in the twin beds in your old room, and Jack—"

"I know. I know. I've got the floor." Jack leaned toward Megan and whispered, "I always do."

Chapter Seven

The next morning came early. It didn't help matters that Jack and the boys started work at daybreak, which by his calculation felt more like three in the morning. A good part of the day was spent pounding posts along the driveway to hang lanterns for the wedding reception.

And, boy, was the driveway long.

Billy had helped too. "Uncle Jack!" he'd shouted at the top of his lungs. "Are you sleeping?"

Jack had raised his head and blinked. *Yes. No. Well, not fully.* "No, I'm awake."

"You don't look awake." Billy wiped his nose with one shirtsleeve.

He was. Jack had been daydreaming about Megan in a bridal veil. Gosh, she was pretty. He didn't think she could get much prettier, but Megan dressed all in wedding white was a picture he couldn't get out of his mind.

Every little sound had kept him awake last night—Steve's snoring, the house settling, and the girls taking turns running to the bathroom in the middle of the night.

"Seems to me you can't fall asleep standing up with your eyes open," Billy said.

" 'Seems to me,' huh?" Jack wondered where his nephew had picked up that new phrasing.

"Yup." Billy resumed orbiting the large oak tree trunk, running a hand over the rough bark.

" 'Seems to me' you've been spending too much time with your grandpa."

Billy asked a lot of questions, which didn't seem to entertain Roy and Andy as much as it did Jack.

"How many more are there?" Billy asked for the twentieth time.

"I don't know. A lot more," Jack answered for the twentieth time, and he pulled the strap of the overalls he'd borrowed from his dad back onto his shoulder.

His dad's work shirt was a little snug on Jack. Too bad he hadn't brought anything but a change of his regular clothes, he thought. He didn't know what he'd been thinking, but he hadn't expected he would be doing *this* much work when he came home for a wedding.

"Here, Uncle Jack." Billy held out a lantern for Jack to hang from the stake.

Roy Latimer, carrying a shovel in one hand and a couple of stakes over one shoulder, passed Jack and Billy on his way down the gravel drive. "Why don't you see what the girls are doing, Billy?"

"Maybe they need some help," Andy added, following right behind Roy with a couple of lamps.

"Girls are no fun," Billy complained.

"Not at your age," Jack said, and he dropped the

sledgehammer onto a stake across from the previous one. "I know, sport."

The Buick rolled down the drive from the house. Robert Meredith stopped the car next to Jack, climbed out, and nodded, admiring the work. "You boys are doing a fine job there. Forty-one down and only eighty-four to go."

Roy and Andy groaned and sagged onto the handles of their tools. Jack shifted his weight from one foot to the other and let his eyelids close. His dad was getting a real kick out of seeing them suffer.

"Where'd the animals go, Grandpa?"

"What's that?"

"Farm animals: the goats, the chickens, the sheep. You had some the last time I was here," Billy said, still looking around.

"We haven't had any stock for a while now."

"Oh . . ." He sounded so disappointed. "I thought they'd still be here." Billy's frown was bigger than those of the three working men put together.

"I'll drop off another stack of stakes and box of lamps down a-ways."

"Thanks, Dad." Jack glanced over at Roy and Andy, who had already gone back to work. The men were all pulling together for the same reason—the wedding reception. Well, all was fair in love and family, and the Latimer boys were about to become family.

Robert eased into his car and drove off.

"Uncle Jack? Are you going to be doing this all day?" Billy scratched his face.

"It's looking that way." Jack picked up another stake and headed for the side of the drive.

"This isn't any fun."

"You can say that again." Jack tapped the stake in with the side of his hammer. "Hey, I've got an idea."

"What?" Billy's eyes widened.

"Come here, sport." Jack motioned him closer. Billy raced to Jack, and he leaned over to whisper in his nephew's ear. "Why don't you . . ."

Megan came stumbling into the kitchen at eight— 6:00 A.M. California time. And she hadn't got much sleep the night before.

"Good morning, dear." Aunty Max was busy clearing the early risers' breakfast dishes off the table.

"Morning, Aunty Max. Let me give you a hand." She picked up a couple of plates and headed for the sink.

"No, I'm fine. Everyone's so busy with the wedding and all, this is something I can do to help. Why don't you sit down and have some breakfast?"

"That'd be great. But I can still help." Megan poured herself a cup of coffee.

"I can manage." Aunty Max waved her in the direction of the work counter. "Well, how about if you start making the ham salad sandwiches for the boys' lunch?"

"Sure." Megan sipped the coffee and wondered when

the last time was she'd had a ham salad sandwich. "Shall I chop the onions?"

"Cutting board's next to the fridge, and the onions are sitting on the counter."

Billy came running to the door, out of breath, and slammed it shut. "Aunty Max, do you know where Aunt Shelley is?" He jumped up and down with excitement.

Aunty Max's eyebrows came together in thought. "Is she in the tent?"

"No."

"Is she out with the girls, collecting ivy? Why don't you check the flower garden?"

"Okay. Thanks." He dashed out of the kitchen twice as fast as he had entered.

Aunty Max chuckled. "What on earth was that about?"

"He seemed in an awful hurry." Megan set an onion on the cutting board and began to chop.

The crunch of gravel outside announced a vehicle pulling up next to the house. "Is that another delivery?" Aunty Max peered out the window. "My word. It's those busybody Brewsters."

The farm tenants.

"They think they can drop in anytime because they live on the same plot of land."

Outsiders. Onion vapors brought tears to Megan's eyes.

"I know they're trying to get an invite to dinner. Don't they realize this is a time for family?"

Megan didn't know what to say. She was an outsider herself.

"Well, I'll teach them a lesson. Fritz!"

The large golden retriever came bounding in from the living room and planted himself at Aunty Max's feet.

"Good boy. You stay." Aunty Max grabbed another dirty plate from the stack next to the sink.

A knock on the door sounded just before it swung open. Megan was getting an idea of what Aunty Max was talking about regarding the Brewsters and their pushiness.

"Hi there, Maxine." The couple stepped inside.

"Hello, Larry, Alice." Aunty Max nodded. "I'd like you to meet Jack's girlfriend, Megan Donnelly."

"Nice to meet you, Megan," they both said.

"Hello." Megan sniffed, blinking away her tears. "I'm sorry, it's the onions."

"How're the wedding preparations coming along?" Larry asked, eyeing the room. For what, Megan wasn't sure.

"Fine, just fine," Aunty Max replied. "There's enough work for everyone. I'm just doing the breakfast dishes, and Megan, here, is making ham salad for dinner. Won't you join us?"

Aunty Max lowered a dirty plate to Fritz. He licked the dried egg yolk and pieces of bacon bits off the plate. She set the newly "cleaned" plate in the cupboard and held a second plate out to the dog.

With horrified expressions on their face, Alice and

Larry couldn't decline the dinner invitation and get out quickly enough.

A glance at Aunty Max told Megan she'd enjoyed pulling a fast one.

Megan laughed between sniffles from the onion fumes. "Did you see the look on their faces?"

"Serves them right," Aunty Max said without sympathy. "They can't just come around here expecting to horn in on family events. It's not like they're part of *our* family. Shouldn't expect us to deal with them at a time like this, can they, Megan?" Aunty Max removed the top plates from the cupboard and set them in the sink for washing.

Aunty Max had included Megan as part of her family. An aching started in her midsection, at the bottom of her heart, and reached way deep down inside.

Family, a real family.

Megan's family was limited. It had been years since her parents had passed. After that it had been only the two of them—she and her brother, Eric. And with his traveling, they didn't see each other much anymore.

To be included by Jack's relatives was unexpected, and she had to admit that never before had *family* felt so good.

An hour later the kitchen had been cleaned up and the ham salad made.

Billy came charging into the kitchen from the family room. "Do you know where Grandma is, Aunty Max?"

"Ellen?" she muttered to herself. "Isn't she with your Aunt Shelley?"

"No, Aunt Shelley is with Mom and the girls. They're doing *girl* stuff." He made an unpleasant face.

"Girl stuff, huh?" Aunty Max smiled up at Megan. "Did you ask Grandpa?"

"Yeah, but he doesn't know where she is." Billy seemed on the brink of tears.

"How about your mom? Or Uncle Jack?"

He threw himself onto a chair in total frustration. "I can't find Grandma anywhere!"

Ellen entered from the same door Billy had only moments before. "'Bout time we started dinner, isn't it?"

"Grandma!" Billy sprang from the chair and rushed to her side.

"Goodness sakes. What is it?" Ellen pulled him close.

"I gotta ask you something."

"All right. Just a moment, dear." She looked expectantly at Aunty Max.

"We'll start making the sandwiches." Aunty Max opened the cupboard and grabbed a handful of plates.

"We need someone to take Billy into town for his tux fitting, and Jack's tux is ready to be picked up," Ellen said.

"You know I can't drive anymore, Ellen." Aunty Max turned to Megan. "But if you'd drive, I can navigate. I certainly know my way around town."

"That would really help us out," Ellen pleaded.

How could Megan say no? "Sure. I don't mind."

"Good. Come with me, Billy." Ellen steered him toward the back door. "We can talk on our way out to tell the boys it's time to eat."

Billy was out the back door before you could say come-and-get-it.

Aunty Max and Megan placed side dishes in the center of the kitchen table. A stack of empty plates sat next to the pile of premade sandwiches.

Fifteen minutes later Jack and the Latimer boys came tromping into the kitchen.

"All right, you fellas, just make sure to knock all the dirt off your boots before you come in, and make sure you've washed up before you sit down," Aunty Max instructed by rote.

That's when Megan caught an eyeful of Jack. Jack in a pair of overalls and a snug shirt that strained across his chest and upper arms.

Good gracious!

Aunty Max sidled up to him. "Look at you! I hadn't realized you grew up to be Mr. America." She gave his biceps a squeeze.

Jack crossed his arms and tried to move out of her reach. "Come on, Aunty Max, you'll make me miss the food!"

Billy had made it to the table before Roy and Andy. He helped himself to a several spoonfuls of Jell-O and a half sandwich.

" 'scuse me, Meg." Jack maneuvered around Megan.

She stepped aside and made room for him but couldn't

swallow. At the sight of Buff Midwestern Jack, Megan could barely manage to breathe.

Jack planted himself in the chair in front of her and helped himself to the salad and sandwiches.

Andy, Roy, and Jack spent few words on who wanted what. They systematically rotated the dishes so everyone got a bit of everything.

Aunty Max stepped behind Jack's chair and ran her hands down his shoulders. "I'd love to stand here and admire you a little longer, but we were just on our way out. Right, Megan? Megan?"

Megan blinked. Her eyes had been open so long, they watered when she got around to closing them. "Yeah, on our way out," she repeated without really knowing what she was saying.

"Well, we'll see you boys when we get back." Aunty Max tugged on Megan's elbow on her way out the door. "This way, dear, remember? The car is out back."

Megan managed to tear her eyes off Jack, put them back into their sockets, then follow Aunty Max out the door.

"We'll take Ellen's car. The keys are in the ignition." Aunty Max headed to the blue coupe.

Megan, still in a haze of Jack, headed off in a different direction.

"Megan? Megan, we're going in this car."

Chapter Eight

Three hours later at the Caldwell Corners Community Church, Megan sat next to Aunty Max in a back pew and watched Jack during the wedding ceremony rehearsal. He wiggled his fingers, getting Megan's attention, and crinkled his nose, blowing her flirting kisses from the sidelines.

No doubt about it, he was a cute one. Adorable.

"If I may please have your attention, we'll get started." The Reverend Mr. Dawes stood at the front, conducting the Latimer-Meredith wedding party. "First, I'll have everyone in the ceremony stand in their final places at the altar. I'll start with the bride and groom."

Jack was all Megan saw. Jack with his adorable dimpled cheeks; Jack and that charming twinkle in his eyes; Jack and his trusting smile . . . Megan had never known there were quite so many different sides to him. There was the warm and understanding Jack she knew and adored; the studly, Gorgeous-George Jack she saw earlier this afternoon; and this latest incarnation, Jack the Jokester.

Soon after Megan had started the car earlier that day

to drive into Caldwell with Aunty Max, Billy came barreling out of the house. Did he go anywhere at less than a dead run?

"Wait for me! Wait for me!" he'd cried, rushing up to them.

"Oh, that's right. Billy's to be fitted for his tux," Aunty Max reminded Megan. "How could we have forgotten?"

Megan knew exactly how *she* had forgotten. One look at Jack, and every thought flew from her mind, that's how.

Billy hopped into the backseat and closed the car door behind him. "Aunty Max, can we stop at the hardware store on the way home?"

"Don't forget to buckle your seat belt, young man," she scolded before coming back to, "Hardware store? Heavens, why do you need to go there?"

Billy managed to take a breath while buckling up, but it didn't stop him from talking. "Uncle Jack said I could get some pony seeds there."

"Pony seeds? What on earth are those?"

"They're seeds you plant, just like soybeans and corn, except they grow into ponies."

Megan met Aunty Max's gaze in mutual disbelief before putting the car into gear and inching away from the house. Without a word, she knew with that look that they'd be humoring Billy.

"Take a right at the road," Aunty Max said, then turned back to Billy. "What's this about growing ponies?"

"Uncle Jack said so. Since Grandpa doesn't have ponies anymore, Uncle Jack said I can grow them myself."

"He did, did he?"

"Look"—Billy held up a dollar bill—"he even gave me some money. He was sure that I could get at least five or six of them."

"Did he, now?" Aunty Max said. "We'll see what we can find, Billy."

The car reached the end of the driveway, and Megan turned right onto the blacktop.

"That Jack," Aunty Max huffed. "I just can't imagine why he would make up something like that. Where does he get it from?"

This from the lady who'd used a golden retriever to "wash" her breakfast dishes in front of the neighbors? There was definitely some weird sense of humor running through the Meredith family.

"Now," the Reverend Mr. Dawes announced, drawing Megan's attention back to the here and now of the church. "We'll practice the entire ceremony from the beginning."

The wedding party wandered back to their starting positions.

"All right, the music will play as Roy and Jack are escorting guests to their seats," the minister narrated. "Come along, guests."

Roy led the way with one family member posing as a guest. Aunty Max grabbed hold of Jack's arm and called to Megan over her shoulder, "Age before beauty."

They were a pair, those two. Megan watched Jack walk Aunty Max down the aisle. Jack might think he was cute and funny now, but she was going to let him have it about lying to Billy about the pony seeds.

Jack watched Aunty Max slide into the second pew and gave Megan the thumbs-up.

His glimpse of Megan standing at the back of the church was not one Jack would soon forget. He could just picture her in a white satin wedding gown and flowing veil of her own instead of the light blue dress she was wearing now.

It would be her turn someday. And he would be the one waiting for her at the altar. Someday.

"Are you a guest of the bride or groom?" Jack asked, offering his arm to her.

"The bride." Megan linked her arm to his as they started down the aisle, and added, "But not the bride's brother."

"What?" He stared at her.

"You're in big trouble, buster."

"Trouble? Why? What did I do?"

Megan stepped into the second row and sat next to Aunty Max.

"Gentlemen, to the back, let's go," the Reverend directed.

Jack came down the aisle with his mother on his arm, but he kept glancing at Megan as he stopped at the first pew. Ellen sat, and Jack retreated.

"Now the music stops and changes, marking the start

of the ceremony." The Reverend Mr. Dawes nodded to Jeff and Andy Latimer, who approached.

At the bottom of the aisle, the junior bridesmaid, Brittney, stepped out first, followed by the matron of honor, Pamela, the flower girls, Sarah and Jennifer, and finally the ring bearer, Billy.

When the wedding party reached the front of the church, the Reverend Mr. Dawes said, "Then the organ will play: dum, dum, da-dum. Shelley and Robert will appear, and everyone will stand."

By that time Jack had made it to the third pew and slid toward the center, sitting just behind Megan and Aunty Max.

Shelley and her father started their long walk down the aisle to the altar.

"What did you mean by—" Jack whispered to Megan. She shushed him.

Jack leaned closer and tried to whisper again.

Megan shushed him louder this time.

"This is like watching a dream come true," Aunty Max whispered with a sigh.

She had said almost the same thing that afternoon as she instructed Megan to take Billy out to the paddock and help him plant and water his pony seeds.

Except the dream, Billy's dream, would turn into a nightmare when morning came and he realized that none of his seeds had sprouted.

Why had she gone along with the lunacy? Megan

knew they were only sunflower seeds, and she knew Billy was in for a big letdown.

Yes, he had had fun. Loads. Billy had been as excited as any boy could be, and equally excited to give Aunty Max a step-by-step description of how he'd dug each and every hole to plant his pony seeds.

"This one's name is Toby," he'd said. "And this one is Bullet, and this one is Sport." He'd covered the seeds one by one just as he had the first three he'd planted. He'd called out each and every one of their names to her: Pal, Lightning, and Thunder. "They might not all grow, you know," he'd told Megan. "Sometimes they don't. But that's just sometimes."

His optimism nearly broke her heart. Megan was somewhat relieved to hear that Billy understood there was a chance that nothing would happen. It might make the ponies' absence in the morning easier for him to accept.

Aunty Max really shouldn't have let it get that far, Megan mused, but Jack had started the whole business.

"You didn't forget to lock the gate, did you?" Aunty Max had reminded Billy after they went in to wash up. "You wouldn't want the ponies running loose after they sprout."

And still Megan had said nothing. She could just kick herself now.

"I will pronounce you man and wife." The Reverend Mr. Dawes' voice rang through the church. "And this is the time when you kiss the bride."

Jeff took Shelley into his arms and kissed her.

"Okay." The minister tapped Jeff on the shoulder. "Save it for the honeymoon. Remember, this is a public ceremony."

Shelley giggled.

"I will introduce you to the guests, there will be applause, and Shelley will take Jeff's arm. Jeff, you will lead your bride down the aisle and into the vestibule."

Shelley linked her arm through Jeff's, and they walked down the aisle, followed by the rest of the wedding party in perfect order.

Megan stood and waited for the wedding party to pass before exiting. If only the real thing went as well tomorrow. She knew that tomorrow morning wasn't going to begin well, because she was certain it would be starting off with their ring bearer in tears.

Jack couldn't wait to have a word with Megan. He kept quiet while riding in the back of his parents' car on their way to the Elks' Lodge for the rehearsal dinner.

Their time would come, his and Megan's. This whole trip was supposed to be their time together. It wasn't quite working out that way. Yet.

He had already spent that entire day with a sledgehammer in one hand and steel stakes in the other. One hundred and twenty-four stakes for one hundred and twenty-four lights lining the driveway for the wedding reception tomorrow night. It was backbreaking work, but deep down inside Jack knew it was worth the effort if it made Shelley happy. But still, he felt guilty for leaving Megan by herself.

Maybe that's why she was mad at him. Still, it wasn't like her to get upset. He'd figured she'd be more understanding than that.

Inside the lodge, the wedding party enjoyed supper, serenaded by a small musical group playing dance-type music in the background.

"Do you want to dance?" Jack had waited all through supper for a chance to be alone with Megan.

"You dance?"

"It happens." Jack shrugged. "Shocking, isn't it?" He led her onto the dance floor and swung her into his arms. She was warm and soft and felt oh-so-good against him. Could this get any better? Jack thought not. All he could do was make it last as long as possible.

"What did you do today?" he asked.

"Not a whole lot," she said matter-of-factly. "I made ham salad sandwiches, and I ran Aunty Max into town for Billy and your tuxes. *You* were busy today."

Megan wasn't saying *that* matter-of-factly. And he had the feeling she wasn't talking about the time he'd spent pounding in lamp stakes. Then what was she miffed about? "Is this part of the 'I'm not a friend of the bride's brother' again?"

"As long as I've known you, I never thought of you as a malicious jokester."

" 'Malicious jokester'?" Jack slapped on the most serious face he could muster. "I haven't a funny bone in my body. Everyone takes me seriously. Completely seriously."

"That's what I'm afraid of." She looked him straight in the eye. "I know about the pony seeds."

" 'Pony seeds'?" he repeated. That was a guilty tone if she'd ever heard one. "You know about that?"

"Billy told us all about it—Uncle Jack and the pony seeds. What a horrible thing to tell him."

"The kid had nothing to do, and he was bored watching me work. His only other choice was to join the girls—that's no choice. I grew up with two sisters; I can completely understand how horrible it is for him. I just wanted to give him something to do, and he had such a great time hunting for 'em." Jack smiled, a smug smile. "It's too bad we were fresh out."

"Aunty Max managed to find some in town today."

"You don't say." A smile touched his eyes, and amusement lifted the corners of his mouth.

"Aunty Max told Billy that they might look like sunflower seeds, but they were really pony seeds."

"Yup, they're remarkably similar," he agreed.

"She told him to plant them in the paddock next to the barn. She made sure Billy latched the gate so the ponies wouldn't get out when they sprouted."

"Good idea," Jack agreed with a nod of his head.

"She also told him they were a new kind—genetically engineered ones that sprout *overnight.*"

Jack stopped and stood motionless on the dance floor. "Overnight?"

Megan watched the play of emotions pass over his face—shock, panic, fear. She could almost see the gears turning in his head. He *should* be scared, horrified of what he was doing to his nephew.

"You can't tell me that Billy isn't going to be disappointed when those seeds haven't sprouted by morning."

"Don't worry." Jack tightened his arm around her waist and drew her near, back into dance position. "I wouldn't dare disappoint him."

Megan felt time stop, freezing the moment between two notes of music while she stared into his eyes. She wasn't sure he was talking about Billy anymore. She had the oddest feeling that Jack was talking about not disappointing *her.*

He gazed into her eyes, a look warm and familiar. His voice whispered, soft and intimate, enticing her nearer. Jack was looking at her in a different way than he ever had before.

Their dancing slowed to nearly a standstill, and he leaned toward her, tilting his face as if . . . she could have sworn he was about to kiss her.

He moved closer, then closer still. . . .

Megan let her breath slip out, realizing that she would let him. If he wanted to, that was.

Then the music stopped, and so did Jack. The moment was lost; he straightened and flashed a smile.

Brittney, Sarah, and Jennifer came rushing toward Megan and pulled her away through the people making their way to and from the dance floor.

"Come on, Aunty Shelley needs to talk to all the girls. Come on! Come on!" they cried.

Jack waved her away. "I'll see you in a couple of minutes." He must have known it was as hopeless to break free from the enthusiastic trio as she did.

Megan watched the bride, Shelley, hold court with the other women of the wedding party. "I want to make sure that everyone knows that after breakfast tomorrow morning we're going on a flower-gathering expedition. Mom and Dad have been nurturing some lovely blooms in their backyard for the reception tables."

The girls sprang to their feet and squealed in excitement. "All right." Pamela tried to quiet them. "We need to get you kids home to bed."

None of the kids' complaints or whines kept Pam or Steve from rounding up the four and herding them out of the Elks' Lodge for home.

"I'm the official babysitter. I'll see you in the morning, dear." Aunty Max kissed Megan on the cheek before leaving.

Shelley made her way to Megan's side. "I want to make sure you'll be joining us tomorrow."

Megan felt a little awkward, as if she were intruding on the family again. But she answered, "Of course I'll be there."

"Good." Shelley smiled, and Megan felt that surge of closeness, of being wanted, wash through her. "I don't want you to miss out."

Megan tossed in bed for the hundredth time, hoping she wouldn't wake Aunty Max in the next bed. Was it impossible that Jack had wanted to kiss her?

The more she thought about it, the more she convinced herself that she must have misunderstood his signals. She'd seen only what she'd wanted to see. There would be no way he'd want to kiss her—she knew he didn't feel that way about her.

Get real, she told herself. This trip was killing her emotionally. Once she got back home, she had to get the ball rolling with . . . with . . . Her mind went blank.

Megan sat straight up in bed, gasping with astonishment. Her new boyfriend—she couldn't remember his name. His name . . . was . . . What was his name?

Blinking into the darkness, Megan nearly panicked. Come on . . . come on . . . How could she forget?

What was his name? B-B-B . . .

Brendon?

Bran-don . . . that was it. Brandon.

She'd only been gone for a day and a half. How on earth could she have forgotten his name? She had to make it work with him, no matter what. Had to.

Brandon.

Megan settled back into bed and closed her eyes,

willing herself to dream about Brandon, not Jack; Brandon's arms around her, not Jack's; Brandon's kisses, not Jack's.

Why hadn't he kissed Megan while he had the chance? Jack had been asking himself all night. He folded the blanket down and crossed his arms, trying to get comfortable on the parlor sofa.

He was such a chicken.

He'd had his arms wrapped around her; he should have just done it. He was a big, stupid chicken.

He would have kicked himself if he weren't lying down. *At the very next opportunity he'd do it*, he promised himself. He wouldn't chicken out anymore; he would kiss her and tell her exactly how he felt about her the very next time they were alone.

He'd find another chance tomorrow. He'd let the wedding atmosphere create a romantic mood, and then he'd tell her.

Chapter Nine

"The ponies! They grew!" Billy screamed, nearly running Megan over in the hallway and plowing down the stairs. "The ponies are here!"

Megan hung on to the banister until he passed her. What was he saying? Ponies? What ponies? Oh, *those* ponies. How could that be?

"For heaven's sake, what is all this noise? What's going on?" Ellen Meredith came into the parlor through the kitchen door, followed by Aunty Max.

"Ponies! Ponies! Billy says there are ponies!" Brittney, Sarah, and Jennifer all squealed and made a mad dash for the front door behind Billy. Again Megan held on to the banister for dear life when the three girls zipped by her.

A few moments passed, then Billy came barreling back in through the front door. "Uncle Jack! Uncle Jack! Where's Uncle Jack?" He made a quick search around his grandmother and Aunty Max before running back out the front door. "Come on, Megan. You have to see!"

She did. Megan had to see these ponies—which had

supposedly sprouted from seeds—with her own eyes. She followed Billy outside.

Whinnies and hoofbeats sounded from the paddock where she had helped Billy plant the seeds. Brittney, Sarah, and Jennifer were feeding several ponies handfuls of grass.

It was true. There were ponies—black and white ones, just as the seeds had been. Megan ran closer until she saw all six ponies chasing one another around and around and . . .

But how did they get here?

Well, of course they didn't really sprout from the ground. She knew better than that.

But then, how did—

"Uncle Jack, you gotta come see!" Billy couldn't drag Jack to the paddock fast enough. "They're here. All of them."

Carrying a small bucket in each hand, Jack allowed Billy to tow him to the fence. "I saw them, Billy. I'm just surprised they all sprouted. Usually there are a couple that don't." Jack's broad smile told Megan that he got more pleasure from Billy's reaction than the botanical miracle.

"There's enough for all us kids to ride. We don't have to take turns or anything." Billy held a dirt-smudged hand out, trying to lure one of the ponies near enough to touch.

"Those new and improved seeds work great. They're much better than the kind I used as a kid." Jack set down his buckets, and his nieces gathered around him. "Which one's your favorite?"

Billy pointed to the smallest one. "Mine's Toby." The girls pointed at each of theirs, and Billy named them off. "That's Pal, that one is Lightning, and his name is Sport."

Staring at Jack, Megan leaned against the top rail and rested her chin on her arms. He's done this. She wasn't sure how, but Megan knew he had. He was awfully quiet, and his smile told her that he was enjoying the ponies as much as the kids.

He handed out carrot pieces from a small pail. "Go ahead and feed them."

"Can we ride them, Uncle Jack?" Billy called out from across the paddock. The girls giggled in agreement.

"We'll need some saddles. I'm sure we can get some over here by this afternoon."

"Afternoon?" the kids whined.

"We have a wedding to get ready for, remember?" their uncle reminded them.

"Oh, yeah, the wedding." Billy hopped off the fence rail, and ran toward the house with his usual flat-out speed.

"Girls, we're supposed to collect flowers for the tables," Jack reminded them.

"The flowers! The wedding!" the girls shrieked, circling around Jack, expending more energy than any adult even after two cups of coffee, before running after Billy.

Jack held out a second bucket to Megan. "I brought this for you."

Megan took the bucket and glanced inside. It was empty. "What's this for?"

"We're going to collect flowers for the wedding." Jack motioned her to follow with a jaunty jerk of his head. "The flower garden is behind the house."

Megan didn't know what to think about Jack anymore. Her once best-platonic-boyfriend seemed to be behaving almost . . . romantically toward her. But that couldn't be right.

They were the first to arrive in the garden. Surrounded on three sides by raised flower beds, Megan stopped in the middle of the fifty-by-fifty-foot-square lawn and took in the sight.

Many tall lilac bushes sported purple and white blooms. Huge pink and white peony bushes lined the sides, framing the shorter perennials and annuals. Behind the peony bushes, multicolored sweet peas twined up trellises, reaching a good eight feet high.

"I'd say there are more than enough flowers, don't you think?" Jack unlocked his garden shears, opening and closing them a few times, getting ready to work. "Pretty amazing, isn't it? Shelley really wanted a home-grown touch, and Mom already had a pretty good flower garden started. They expanded the garden a year ago when Shell got engaged."

"Let me put some water into that bucket." Jack took Megan's bucket and headed over to the garden hose.

Strolling to the far end of the raised bed, Megan found a patch of herbs. Easily identifiable were mint, thyme, parsley, and chives, along with a couple she didn't recognize. She pinched a sprig of rosemary, inhaling the scent.

"You have to smell this." She held the sprig toward him, up to his nose. "Nice, isn't it? We don't have this with our apartment living."

Jack held her hand still, doing his best to bring Megan closer to him. "Hmmm. It smells so good"—he stared into her eyes—"they should call it Rose*Megan.*"

He'd pulled her closer to him very slowly, then leaned toward her even more slowly. The look on his face . . . in his eyes . . .

It was happening again. That feeling . . . he was going to kiss her. Megan didn't want to break the spell; she wanted it to happen.

"Ponies? Ponies?" Shelley shrieked, stalking into the flower garden.

Megan pulled back and was only a reflex behind Jack, who'd already shot up straight.

"This is all your fault, Jack! What were you thinking? Are you crazy? I don't want a bunch of hairy animals prancing around at my wedding."

"Well, you should have thought of that before you invited Jeff's brothers." Jack laughed.

"This isn't funny. Don't you think I'm under enough stress as it is?" Shelley pressed a palm to her forehead, then rubbed her eyes. "I don't know if I'm going to make it through today."

"Shell, relax." Jack pulled his sister to him and draped an arm around her. "The ponies aren't going to get in the way. In fact, they'll keep the kids entertained during the reception."

Jack turned Shelley back toward the house and gravitated back in that direction. "Don't worry. Everything's going to be fine. You'll see."

Brittney came sprinting down the stretch of lawn toward them. "I won! I'm first." She stopped when she'd reached the center and raised her arms in triumph, swinging her bucket over her head.

Megan had kept quiet and out of the way during the sibling skirmish. Jack looked at her now, and she looked at him. Whatever she thought might have happened before Shelley's arrival wasn't going to have a second chance at happening.

"You're first, the worst, and I'm next, the best," Sarah proclaimed when she reached the imaginary finish line. Jennifer dashed in a few moments later, and Sarah told her, "You're third, the nerd."

"You brat. I am not a nerd," Jennifer sassed back. "Mom!"

Pamela, with more empty buckets in hand, arrived after the girls.

"Okay, that's enough." Shelley did her best to end the squabbling.

"Please try to remember why we're here." Pamela glanced around, visually accounting for her chicks. "Where's Billy gone?"

"I thought he was with you," Jack replied.

"No, he went back to be with the ponies," Brittney said in that tattletale tone. "He should be out here working with us."

"Let's put a little bit of water into those buckets before we set the flowers in, shall we?" Pamela motioned the girls toward the house.

"Let me give you a hand, Jennifer." Megan motioned her over.

Ellen walked to the clearing, waving to catch someone's attention. "Shelley, Hilda just called from the salon and said she's packing up her curling iron and is on her way. You'd better hurry if you want that relaxing bubble bath that you've been talking about for the last six months."

"My bubble bath!" Shelley's composure flew out the window. "I almost forgot all about that." She edged by Megan and Pamela with a polite "Excuse me" and raced back to the house.

Pamela turned to Megan. "All those bridal magazines recommend the bride take time to pamper herself, but there just isn't enough time. Remember that when your time comes."

"Now remember, Brittney," Megan reminded Pamela's eldest while capping the nail polish. "Don't touch anything until your nails have dried."

"I won't." Brittney held her hands up in admiring fashion. She spread her fingers out in front of her, making sure nothing would touch her freshly painted nails. "Look, Aunt Shelley. It's such a pretty pink. This is going to look so great with my dress."

Hilda, the hairdresser, had finished rolling Shelley's hair and had switched over to style Pamela's. Diane, Hilda's assistant, had just finished doing Pamela's nails and was starting Shelley's manicure.

"How are you two doing?" Megan asked Sarah and Jennifer, who sat perfectly still to one side, waiting for their nails to dry. "Your polish should be dry by now."

Aunty Max set aside the magazine she'd been reading and stood. "All right, then, let's go downstairs. Your grandma has a project for you girls."

"Are we going to—" Jennifer began.

Aunty Max herded them to the kitchen. "You'll see when you get there."

Even with wet nails, Brittney made it to the door first and still managed to complain, "I can't. My fingernails are still wet."

"Then you'll lend a hand when they dry," Aunty Max pronounced.

"Well, I guess this is the last wedding for your family for a while, isn't it?" Diane finished shaping the nails on one of Shelley's hands and started on the other.

"Could be." Pamela sighed and didn't do a very good job at stifling her grin.

"Well, there's always . . ." Shelley trailed off, but her smile lingered.

Megan noticed the abrupt silence and couldn't help but notice Shelley and Pamela's stares slowly turning toward her. She could feel Jack's name hanging unspoken in the air.

Shelley and Pamela went wide-eyed when a car pulled up to the house. "It's another delivery," Hilda announced, looking out the window.

Shelley's earlier excitement at her big day's finally being here had given way to panic at the introduction of Jack's ponies and had now evolved into near indifference. It was pretty clear that she was tired of the preparations and ready to get on with the wedding itself.

Megan had finished cleaning up after polishing the girls' nails. "I can run downstairs and take care of it if you'd like."

"Would you mind?" Shelley asked, sounding relieved. Diane had hold of her hand, and Hilda had Pamela by a strand of hair. There was no way either of them could handle a delivery. "Just point them to the tent."

"I'm on it." Megan headed out the door, turned left at the hall, and went down the stairs. Reaching the main floor, she froze when she heard her name.

"You wouldn't believe how good she is with Billy— all the kids, really." It was Ellen's voice. "He had such a good time with her yesterday."

"I know, Mom. Megan's great." That was Jack's voice. Jack's mom was picking on him.

"She's going to make such a wonderful mother

someday." Now Aunty Max's voice chimed in. "Don't you dare let her get away. You want to hang on to that girl."

"I know, Aunty Max. I know. I'm working on it." He sounded tired, drained, as if he'd been fending them off for some time. And they were ganging up on him . . . about her. It wasn't fair.

Poor Jack. Of course he was going to agree with anyone and everyone who pressed him. What else could he say? He wasn't about to tell them the truth—that they weren't really a couple.

"Grandma!" one of the girls shrieked from the kitchen in urgency.

"Coming," Ellen responded.

It went quiet, and Megan heard the kitchen door swing. She couldn't resist taking a peek at Jack, and she leaned around the corner just a little.

The doorbell rang again. With all the activity that morning, it was a wonder that the bell hadn't worn itself out.

"I'll get it," Megan called out, nearly forgetting why she'd come downstairs in the first place. She pushed off the bottom step and strode to the door.

"Well, for goodness sake. Who is that?" Aunty Max asked, joining Megan at the front door.

There stood the best man, Andy Latimer. He had a large smile and a small white box with a wide white gold-edged ribbon tied into a large bow. "This is for the bride, from the groom."

"A present! I just love presents," Aunty Max said over Megan's shoulder. She gave Megan a gentle push, urging her to take the gift.

Megan took the box and guaranteed with a decisive nod that it was in her protective custody. "I'll make sure she gets it."

With his duty completed, Andy turned around and headed back to the car.

Aunty Max nudged Megan toward the stairs. "Well, let's deliver it and see what's inside. Let's have Shelley open it right away."

If Aunty Max was half this insistent about Jack's marrying *her,* Megan's nearly lifelong wish might come true. Although that wouldn't be exactly the way she wanted it.

"This is for you." Megan handed Shelley the small, jewelry-sized box.

Shelley read the attached card and smiled. "It's from Jeff."

Hilda, Diane, Pamela, and Aunty Max gathered around Shelley. Megan had to admit she was equally curious, and she stepped closer to get a peek.

Shelley opened the box, and tears filled her eyes. She pulled out what looked like strung Cheerios and cradled the strand as if it were a necklace of priceless pearls.

"Oh, isn't that sweet," Aunty Max cooed. "When Jeff was eight, he gave her a cereal necklace, and I think they've been in love ever since."

Megan stared at Aunty Max in disbelief. Maybe this

entire family really *did* have a breakfast cereal history. "Does that mean we're really going to throw . . . *puffed rice?*"

Aunty Max sighed and swiped a tear away from her eye. "Shelley wouldn't have it any other way."

Megan was dressed and ready. She smoothed the skirt of her "wedding dress" and made her way down the stairs. She called the shell-pink Alençon lace top with chiffon skirt her "wedding dress" because it was the outfit she always wore to weddings. Other people's weddings.

"Hello? Anyone home?" It was a familiar voice. It sounded almost like her brother, Eric, but someone who would walk into the Meredith house must have been another relative of theirs.

"Eric, is that you?" Ellen called from the kitchen.

Eric? Megan's brother, Eric?

Megan froze on the staircase and stared into the parlor. There was Ellen Meredith, dressed in her ivory mother-of-the-bride suit, hugging someone who looked a lot like Megan's brother, Eric, from the back.

Feeling a bit unreal, Megan stepped into the room. "Eric?"

"Goodness, Megan!" Eric ran toward Megan and couldn't wrap his arms around her fast enough. "What are you doing here?"

"What am *I* doing here? What are *you* doing here?"

Jack had never said anything to Megan about Eric's attending the wedding.

"*Moi?* I'm the official wedding photographer."

"I'm—I'm . . . stunned. I didn't think you did weddings anymore." Dressed in a well-fitted, black, single-breasted tuxedo with a miniature ivory rose tucked into his jacket lapel, he was certainly dressed for the occasion.

"I don't usually—only for special people." Eric threw Mrs. Meredith a glance. Obviously, as his best friend's mom, she was special to him.

Ellen glanced from one to the other. "I'm sorry. I just assumed you both knew."

"I'm afraid not," Eric replied.

"I had no idea," Megan said at the same time.

"Why don't I leave you two alone to catch up? I'll go upstairs and tell Shelley you've arrived."

"Tell her I'm all set up and waiting for her in the back garden." Eric led Megan to the sofa and sat. "Don't tell me you came with Jack."

Megan shrugged. "I came with Jack."

"So is something going on between you two that I should know about?" Eric winked and grinned.

"We—" Megan began, but Mr. Meredith's arrival cut her short.

"Hey, Eric, how you doing?" Dressed in a dark suit and tie, Robert definitely looked like the proud father of the bride.

Eric stood to greet him. They shook hands, and Robert gave him a solid clap on the back.

"You still holding on to Ellen's Thanksgiving turkey?" Robert patted Eric's belly.

"Nice to see you, Mr. Meredith. Thank you for inviting me," Eric returned.

"Thank you for doing this for Shelley. She wasn't going to be satisfied with any other photographer."

"They all say that!" Eric laughed.

"Ellen's gone up to tell her you're here. Is there something else I can do?"

"Be a good fellow and round up the other family members. I'll need them in about twenty out back."

"You got it." Robert headed back toward the stairs.

The kitchen door swung open.

"Ah! Here's the handsome brother of the bride." Eric eyed Jack from the carefully combed hair on the top of his head, down the length of his tailored light gray stroller, to his polished black shoes.

Jack looked breathtakingly handsome. Of course, he had always looked comfortable in a suit and tie. He should: he wore one to work every day. Megan wasn't sure if it was the smart vest, striped slacks, or the black shoes that made the incredible difference today.

Barely a moment passed before voices and rustling sounds approached and Shelley entered the room in a swish and swirl of soft white tulle.

"Here comes the bride!" Eric announced. "And what an absolutely radiant bride she is."

"Eric, you charmer." Shelley and Eric embraced with great care, and he air-kissed her cheeks.

"Don't want to crush your lace." He plucked some nonexistent something off her sleeve, smoothed the line of her satin skirt, and smiled. "Truly, you are a sight to behold." He eyed every inch of her dress with delight. "I'm not sure even *I* can do you justice."

"You're the best, and you know it," Shelley scolded playfully.

"Shall we begin, then?" Eric held out his arm to Shelley. "I've set up in the back garden. Let's not forget the flowers!" he called over his shoulder before stepping out the front door.

"I'll get the bouquets and meet you in the back." Ellen headed toward the kitchen, where the finished flowers were.

In the back garden, Eric had set up his tripod, camera, and three reflectors. He centered Shelley in front of a raised planter with several peony bushes just behind her and lovely greenery providing a lush backdrop for the bridal portrait.

Eric knelt and arranged her skirt symmetrically around her feet. "You're really going through with this? Marrying another man?"

"You had your chance," Shelley replied, still smiling.

"Flirt," he teased, returning the grin. Then he stood to work on her flyaway veil, coaxing it around her face and shoulders until he was satisfied with the way it draped. "What . . . is this?" His smile faded, replaced by an unsatisfied grimace. He raised an eyebrow and pointed at the strand of Cheerios circling her neck, not daring to touch it. "It's not something old, new, borrowed, or blue."

She placed a protective hand over her necklace. "It's sentimental."

Eric took a couple of steps back toward his camera, clearly still puzzling over the homemade jewelry. "I'm not sure edible wheat products work as a bridal accessory."

"Just take the picture," Jack urged from the sidelines.

"Here you go." Ellen handed Shelley her bridal bouquet.

Eric positioned the flowers and her arms. "Hold it low and just a tad forward, would you? Perfect. Now, don't move a muscle." He stepped back to his camera, checked the settings, and met her eyes. He smiled at Shelley and held up one hand, poised to take the picture. "Can you say, 'Happily ever after'?"

Chapter Ten

Megan arrived at the quaint church at 4:45 in the afternoon. Just as rehearsed, Jack walked her down the aisle. Unlike being at the rehearsal, she was totally unprepared for her reaction to walking down the aisle with Handsome Jack dressed to the nines.

She was living out a fantasy she knew could never materialize: she, the beautiful Princess Bride, and he, her Prince Charming.

Megan could feel Jack's strong arm under her hand. And she savored every precious moment until he stopped at the second pew.

Just as rehearsed, she slid in and sat next to Aunty Max. It might have been the same place Megan had been a day ago, but it did not feel the same.

At the end of every pew hung a floral decoration. The altar, bathed in warm candlelight, was ready for the momentous occasion of serving as the backdrop for two people who promised to spend their lives together. Friends and family would witness the bride and groom's promises.

Church organ music pulsed through the air, signaling the beginning of the ceremony.

The Reverend Mr. Dawes, the groom, and the best man entered from the side. They stopped at the altar and looked past the guests, down the aisle.

The music stopped, then changed. Brittney, the junior bridesmaid, began her journey down the aisle. She'd been so very proud to be first. Her mother, Pamela, the matron of honor, followed. Next Sarah and Jennifer looked adorable stepping down the aisle, side by side, in matching dresses. They stopped at the altar, taking their places next to their mother.

Finally the usually exuberant Billy waited calmly until it was his turn, then strode solemnly down the aisle. With not a single hair out of place or wrinkle in his miniature tux, he carried his silk pillow proudly before him and stopped exactly where he was supposed to, to everyone's amazement, directly on his mark.

This was almost too good to be true. Megan wondered what had happened to the real Billy. Last night at the rehearsal, he'd been everywhere except where he was supposed to be, running up and down the aisle, hiding behind the pews, playing hide-and-seek with everybody. Today Billy was behaving like an absolute angel.

The organ's rendition of the traditional "Here Comes the Bride" played. Megan stood with the rest of the guests when Robert and Shelley Meredith arrived for their trip down the aisle.

Jeff Latimer waited at the altar, looking happy, proud, and maybe a little bit scared. His eyes widened and his smile grew when he saw Shelley appear at the back of the church. He watched every step she took toward him. Robert gave Shelley's hand to Jeff and took his seat next to Ellen in the first pew.

"Dearly beloved," the Reverend Mr. Dawes began, his tone reflecting the seriousness of the occasion. "We have come together in the presence of God to witness and bless the joining together of this man and this woman in Holy Matrimony."

Those words . . . *Holy Matrimony.* Would it ever happen for her? Megan wondered if she'd ever have a wedding of her own.

"Jeffrey, will you have this woman as your wedded wife?" The minister's words filled the church.

If Megan never moved past her infatuation for Jack, she'd never be anyone's wife.

"To live together in God's ordinance in the holy estate of matrimony? Will thou love her, comfort her, honor, and keep her, in sickness and in health, and, forsaking all others, keep thee only unto her, so long as you both shall live?"

"I will."

Who would make those promises to Megan? Not Jack. Would any man? Tears filled her eyes, threatening to spill at the sad thought.

Aunty Max pressed a tissue into Megan's hand and whispered, "That's all right, dear. I always get weepy at weddings."

Megan hadn't—not before this one.

"Who gives this woman to be married to this man?"

Ellen and Robert together replied, "We do."

"Shelley and Jeffrey, will you please join hands?" the Reverend Mr. Dawes instructed solemnly.

The muffled weeping around her made Megan feel more like crying with every passing minute, and thoughts of the unattainable kept coming into her mind.

What she wouldn't give to hear the man she loved promise to keep her from this day forward, for better, for worse, for richer, for poorer, in sickness and in health, to love and to cherish, till death us do part.

Shelley's words, "I thee wed," echoed through the church.

Megan pressed the tissue to the corner of her eye, catching her tears before they trickled down her face.

Jack stood at the back of the church to seat any late-comers. He crossed to the groom's side so he could get a clear view of Megan. The bride was supposed to be the most beautiful woman at the wedding, but Shelley would have been disappointed to learn that he thought Megan far outshone her.

That soft pink was the perfect color for Megan. It brought out the darkness of her hair and the rosiness in her cheeks. He could see her eyes glisten, sparkling, from where he stood. She was beautiful. And what an even lovelier bride she would make.

Then she blotted her eyes. Was she crying? He looked harder, watching her every move. Again she brought a tissue to her face.

Were they tears of sadness or joy? Or maybe it was just a woman thing; most of the women here were crying.

"May I have a token of your sincerity that you will keep these vows?"

Pamela handed Jeff's ring to Shelley, who handed it to the minister.

Jeff turned to his best man, Andy, who for a moment stood motionless, then shrugged.

"It's on the pillow; Billy has it." He nodded toward Billy, where the attention of the wedding party, the family, and all the guests settled. In the quiet that followed, everyone could hear Andy say, "Isn't the ring bearer supposed to carry the rings?"

Maybe men didn't know that the real wedding rings were never on the pillow. Shelley's eyes went wide. It'd be a memorable ceremony for all if her ring was missing: the bride strangling the best man.

Jeff motioned Billy forward. He untied the ribbon and took Shelley's gold band off the pillow.

The Reverend Mr. Dawes cleared his throat and held up the rings. "The perfect circle of a ring symbolizes eternity. . . ."

Jack let the words of love, of promise, of commitment soak in. What he wouldn't give to hear Megan make those promises to him.

Anything. Everything.

Would they ever make it that far? He hadn't even kissed her yet. He glanced over at Megan again, and he could feel the nervousness in his stomach. But he would kiss her, he promised himself. They'd be on their way home tomorrow, which meant he had to make his move soon. Before this day was done, Jack was going to tell her how he felt.

"I now pronounce you husband and wife. Those whom God has joined together, let no man put asunder. You may kiss the bride."

Looking happier than Jack had ever seen them, Shelley and Jeff turned toward each other and kissed.

The Reverend Mr. Dawes turned the bride and groom toward the guests and said, "Ladies and gentlemen, may I introduce Mr. and Mrs. Jeffrey Latimer."

Mr. and Mrs. Jeffrey Latimer marched down the aisle to Mendelssohn's "The Wedding March," the wedding attendants followed accordingly, and the guests filed out of the church row by row.

Megan caught a glimpse of the family and the members of the wedding party returning to the altar for formal pictures. Everyone but Jack. He'd followed her outside, to the front of the church.

"Don't you have to take pictures with your family?" she asked.

"I'm sure they can start without me. Besides, I want to make sure—"

"Hey, Jack! They're waiting on you!" someone called from the doorway.

"In a minute," he replied. Then he turned to Megan before taking off. "Snag me a cone, okay?"

"A cone?" Megan whispered to herself. She didn't think he'd been talking ice cream, had he?

True, the weather was growing warmer by the minute, and it almost felt like rain. She'd forgotten how fast the weather could change here. Clear and hot one minute, dark and wet the next. All they needed now was a tornado to drop out of the sky. It couldn't, though—not on Shelley and Jeff's wedding day.

Ten minutes later Sarah, Brittney, and Jennifer came out of the church carrying baskets and meandered through the crowd. Sarah handed Megan a paper cone and continued on to the other guests.

Jennifer handed her a second one. "Here's one for Uncle Jack."

Each cone was filled with Rice Krispies. Megan smiled. Inside the top edge of the cone, in gold script, was written: *Shelley and Jeffrey.*

Billy bumped against Megan's leg while digging into his half-empty cone, eating the contents one grain at a time.

"No, dear." Aunty Max laid a hand on his shoulder. "They're not for eating; they're to throw at your Aunt Shelley and Uncle Jeff."

Billy strained to look up Aunty Max's four-foot-ten height and said, "But I don't have an Uncle Jeff."

"You do now. That's why we had the wedding ceremony."

"It is?" He tilted his head, wrinkling his nose as he stared up at her.

"That's right," Aunty Max answered.

"We throw breakfast at Aunt Shelley and Uncle Jeff?"

"That's right," Aunty Max repeated.

"And then what happens?"

"And then you'll go to Grandma and Grandpa's and ride the ponies."

"The ponies! Come on, Megan." He pulled on her arm before taking off at a run for the church doors, spilling some of the cereal out of the cones she held in her hand. "We're going to ride the ponies!"

"Not now, Billy." Aunty Max calmed him. "We have to wait for the bride and groom to leave first."

Billy ran up the church stairs and screamed inside, "Aunt Shelley, hurry up! We're gonna ride the ponies!"

"Hey, Billy." Jack snagged his nephew at the doorway and walked him back toward Megan and Aunty Max. "Hang on, sport. What's going on?"

"I want those guys to hurry up, Uncle Jack. I want to go home and ride the ponies."

"Yeah, but we can't leave right now." Jack stopped next to Megan.

"We can't?" Confusion clouded Billy's face.

"We just have to eat our cereal and wait until they come out." Jack snagged a couple of pieces from Aunty Max's cone and tossed them into his mouth. She threw him a disagreeable look.

"Did I tell you what a great job you did in there?" Jack laid a hand on his nephew's shoulder.

Billy stuffed a couple of morsels into his mouth and mumbled, "Yeah?"

"Oh, yeah. Didn't he do a great job, Megan?"

"He was perfect," she agreed.

"The best part was how carefully you carried Aunt Shelley's wedding ring on your pillow." Jack wiped invisible sweat off his brow. "If you'd lost that, it would have been the end of the whole ceremony."

"It would?" Billy asked, wide-eyed.

Jack nodded. "No ring, no wedding. You saved the day."

"Wow." Billy certainly seemed impressed with himself and his accomplishment.

"If you could just hang in there for a few more minutes, we'll be on our way back to the farm, and then it'll be pony rides until bedtime."

"Okay, Uncle Jack. I can do that."

"Great, buddy. Great." Jack patted Billy on the shoulder and straightened. "Is one of those mine?"

"Sorry. Here." Megan handed him a cone.

The church bell began to ring.

"Saved by the bell," Jack said; then he looked away from Megan and back again. "I've always wanted to say that. Look—"

A black horse-drawn carriage pulled up at the end of the church walk. Moments later Shelley and Jeff appeared in the doorway. Through a shower of puffed rice, they dashed to the horse-drawn carriage and made their escape.

Amid the smiles and love and cheering and flying breakfast cereal, Megan had a handful of Rice Krispies clasped in one hand and Jack holding her other. His larger, warmer hand surrounded hers, making Megan feel safe and wanted.

If only it could be like this forever.

Megan walked toward the huge white canvas reception tent. She'd seen the tent on her arrival Thursday afternoon, but this was the first time she'd stepped inside. It was as large as a circus tent, and with the kids' voices and laughter and the hoofbeats of the ponies in the background, she half expected to see a clown darting out of the opening.

"Uncle Jack! Megan! Look at me!" Billy yelled from atop a black and white pony in the paddock. "I'm riding Toby!"

"All right, cowpoke!" Jack returned, waving an imaginary cowboy hat in the air.

"Uncle Jack!" the girls chorused. "Look at us!"

"You kids having a good time?"

"Yeah!" they screamed, making Megan happy that they were a good fifty or so feet from ear range.

"Are you and Megan going to ride too?" Billy yelled.

Jack chuckled. "Thanks for the offer. I think we're a little too big for that." He waved at the kids and continued toward the tent.

Inside, tiny lights, some twinkling, hung far overhead, casting a magical glow. Rose and hydrangea centerpieces sat atop the dozens of large round tables draped in white linen. Delicate china place settings, highly polished silverware, and cut crystal added gold and sparkle.

Off to the right, the wedding cake sat on a white linen-tulle–covered table. A hand-blown glass frame perched atop the cake with a picture of a much younger Shelley, wearing a Cheerios-strung necklace, and Jeff, at age eight or so.

Megan watched the guests gather around one side of the tent. "What's going on over there?"

Jack looked over his shoulder. "Oh, that? The guests are pinning up pictures."

"Pictures? What kind of pictures?"

He led the way, heading toward the group. "Everyone was asked to bring pictures they had of Shelley or Jeff growing up."

They neared one of the six-by-eight-foot corkboards displaying old photos. Jack pointed at a picture of a bunch of kids sitting side by side with their feet in a sandbox. "This one is Jeff with the neighbor kids, Glen and Garland Armstrong, Ron Chaney, Jim, Cheryl, and Sammy Ford—and that's Jeff and his brothers, Andy and Roy."

"How old are they?"

" 'Bout ten or so. And this one is Shelley and Jeff picking berries near the creek during summer vacation." He pointed to a third picture. "There's Shelley and Jeff with their friends Susie and Scott just before the junior prom."

Shelley and Jeff were a dozen years younger, but the expression in their eyes didn't look any different from the expressions Megan had seen today. They still loved each other, even after all these years.

"They've known each other nearly their whole lives.

They were childhood and high school sweethearts. After college, we weren't surprised when they started talking about marriage."

Megan stared at a picture of an adorable wavy-haired boy with a dimpled smile surrounded by three little girls. "Is that you?"

Jack exhaled and grimaced in exasperation. "I told Aunty Max not to bring that one. I hate that picture."

Jack looked precious. All cute and adorable.

"You can't see it in the picture, but we were playing dress-up and all wearing puffy slips and Aunty Max's high heels. It was just before Pamela put lipstick on all of us."

Megan widened her eyes and stared at him. "No, you can't see that, but thanks for letting me know."

"All right, folks. If I may have your attention please," a man's deep voice announced over the loudspeaker. Megan supposed he was the DJ. "I've been told to ask people to find their seats; supper will be starting soon."

"Come on." Jack took Megan by the hand. He pulled out a chair to seat her.

There was small gold box tied with a red ribbon sitting on each napkin.

Jack lifted his gold box and said, "Chocolate?"

"I wouldn't be surprised it if was a small box of cereal."

"Maybe it's a chocolate-covered cereal." He sounded hopeful.

One of the waiters stepped between them and filled their Champagne glasses.

Megan glanced at Shelley at the head table. She

hadn't noticed at the church, but Shelley's wreath shimmered and sparkled like tiny, twinkling stars shining around her head.

"Does this thing work?" Robert Meredith said into the cordless black microphone. The guests quieted. "I guess so. Everyone's looking at me like I've got something important to say."

Some of the guests laughed, and there was an anonymous, "Okay, Bob, let's hear it," shouted from the crowd, amid the general rumblings of people talking and making comments to one another.

Robert chuckled and cleared his throat. "I'd like to thank everyone for coming. Today is Shelley and Jeff's big day. Ellen and I are delighted that so many dear friends and relatives from both families—who are too numerous to name—have joined in our celebration. Wasn't that a beautiful ceremony?"

The guests nodded and voiced their agreement.

"I know you all want me to sit down so we can start supper, but as father of the bride, I have my duty. I'd like you all to join me in wishing the couple well."

The guests held their Champagne glasses aloft throughout the tent, ready for the toast.

"Ladies and gentlemen, to the health, happiness, and prosperity of the newlyweds"—Robert raised his glass—"Shelley and Jeff."

The guests clinked their glasses and repeated the toast, "To Shelley and Jeff!"

Chapter Eleven

Supper had ended for pretty much everyone after an hour had passed. Andy Latimer stood, and the room's noise level quieted to a respectable din.

"It's my turn to say a few words, 'cause I'm the best man. And what I really want to know is, if I'm the best man, why isn't Shelley marrying me instead of my brother?"

A rumble of laughter roved around the room.

Was that the oldest best-man joke in the world, or what? Not that Jack could have done any better. He was just glad *he* wasn't the brother who had to stand and make a speech.

"I guess I should be grateful to have Shelley as a sister-in-law." Andy slid a hand into his pocket, shifted his weight to one leg, and continued. "Before we get on with the festivities, I just wanted to say, Jeff, Shelley"— he turned to them—"I think I can speak for most of the guests when I say, *It's about time!* We've waited nearly twenty years for you two to get married."

The guests roared, cheered, and hooted, whole-heartedly agreeing with the statement.

Jeff stood. "Thanks, Andy. I have to admit that, Shelley, marrying you is better than I ever imagined. Thank you, everyone, for making our wedding day special." He lifted his Champagne glass. "I toast you all. To our family and friends. All right, everyone, let's have a good time." Jeff helped Shelley stand, and they waved at their guests to a response of thunderous applause.

As if on cue, people started to talk, the catering staff collected dirty dishes from the tables, and others poured more Champagne.

"Now that the speeches are over, we can get to the fun stuff." Jack rubbed his hands together in anticipation.

"Stay away from the cake," Megan warned. "Shelley will kill you if you sneak a bite."

"Cake? Who said anything about cake?"

Megan sat back and crossed her arms. "I know how you are around food." He could probably smell the butter cream from the far end of the tent.

Now what? Jack wondered. How was he to tell the woman of his dreams that he loved her? Where was his confidence, his charisma, his charm when he needed it?

Who was he kidding? He didn't have any of those things.

Okay. He'd have to wing it—pretend he was suave, dashing, and worldly. Be cool, subtle, about expressing his feelings for her. Ease into the subject. That was it, slow and easy.

"Hey, lovebirds." Eric broke in between them with the

long lens on a 35mm camera in one hand and a glass of Champagne in the other. "Do you think I could get a picture of you two together? I just want a shot of my two favorite people for my scrapbook." He looked from Jack to Megan and said, all singsong-y, "I promise I'll send you a copy."

"Sure, glad to." Jack smiled and stood, holding Megan's hand. They followed Eric away from the tables to the far side of the dance floor. "Here . . . Jack, put your arms around her waist, and, Meggers, drape your arms around his neck. Now . . . slow dance."

"But they're playing a mambo," Megan complained. An upbeat salsa tune throbbed in the background.

"Pre*tend*." Eric pleaded for her cooperation. "Use your imagination."

Megan slid her arms around Jack's neck and stepped close, resting her head against his chest. Jack splayed his hands on her back; she felt soft and warm in his arms. He couldn't get over how wonderful, how right, it felt. Perfect.

He brushed his cheek against her soft hair. It had a clean, fresh, light scent.

Megan followed his lead, swaying slowly to the imagined music, mimicking a slow dance.

"Wonderful." Eric clicked away, encouraging them. "Don't look at me, look at each other."

Jack had a hard time relaxing. It wasn't as if he played fashion model on a regular basis. But looking into Megan's familiar, warm, comforting eyes soon made him forget his discomfort, and everything around him faded away.

"This isn't a high school dance. Shake it up. Let's see some steam," Eric urged with a shimmy. "Let's see some sizzle."

Sizzle? Jack couldn't—not here, not in front of everybody.

"Sparks!" Eric urged. "*SIZ*-ZLE!"

Jack froze, unsure what to do. Until Megan gazed into his eyes. The way she looked into his eyes made him feel he could do just about anything.

Click, click, click.

Her eyes were smoldering and inviting. . . . She'd never looked at him that way before. Ever. And he liked it.

"Now we're cooking with gas!" Eric announced from what sounded like some far-off place.

Click, click, click.

Eric lowered the camera. "Could you at least *pretend* to enjoy yourself just a little bit, Jack?" he said sarcastically.

Click, click, click.

"All right, folks," the DJ's voice broke in, quieting the room. "It's time to cut the cake! If everyone will gather around, we'll get a sample of Shelley and Jeff's table manners. Will they be nice, or will they start a food fight?"

Click, click, click.

"Okay, you can stop. That's it. We're done," Eric announced. "Got to go. Duty calls."

Jack could see a crowd already heading toward the cake table. When cake was involved, he wanted to be the first one in line. Actually, he wanted to jump ahead of the line.

Megan followed in Jack's path toward the wedding cake. He was the bride's brother, but still . . . "Um, I think you have to stand in line, just like everyone else."

"Oh, yeah?" He nodded and took her by the hand, as if he were accepting a challenge. "We'll see about that."

Eric snapped pictures of the bride and groom posing with the cake, the bride and groom with the cake knife, and the bride and groom with the cake *and* the knife. They finished the ceremony by cutting the cake and feeding each other a polite taste.

No more than two minutes later Jack stood at Megan's side with a generous piece of cake.

"You've got to try this," he said through a mouthful. "It's really good. I brought you a fork so we can share. I snagged us a big piece."

"If it's food, you'll like it," Megan announced.

Roy Latimer approached them in a stealthlike maneuver and whispered, "The bluebird flies at dawn," while glancing over his shoulder, then strolled nonchalantly away.

"What was that about?" Megan had no idea.

Jack leaned forward. "He's talking about the secret mission."

"Secret mission?" Jack's family was a loveable one,

but, she had to admit, in their way, a bit odd. Apparently one could be affected even when one married into it.

Outside the tent, they met up with Roy and Brittney. Roy handed Megan and Jack each a long candle lighter and led them to the driveway.

"You know why we're all here." Roy looked each of them in the eye in turn, completely serious.

Megan glanced from Brittney, standing on her left, to Jack on her right. "I don't."

"We're here to light the candles," Brittney whispered back.

"Candles on the driveway, okay." Megan could go along with that.

"All you do is turn the safety off and put the lighter in the jar"—Roy demonstrated on the nearest candle—"pull the trigger on the lighter, and light the candle. Easy."

"Megan and I will start at the oak tree and work our way to the blacktop," Jack said to Roy.

"Gotcha. Brittney and I will start here and work our way in toward the tree. See you back at the tent after we complete the mission."

All this top-secret planning was silly but did make the task fun. Thank goodness Roy didn't go so far as to have them synchronize their watches before splitting up.

Megan walked with Jack down the driveway past his parents' house, past the old barn, past all the cars parked in one of the pastures, and finally past the nickering ponies in the paddock.

"Sorry about the cloak-and-dagger stuff," Jack said. "Roy's ex-military."

The warm afternoon had given way to a cool evening. Stars twinkled in between the clouds floating overhead, not unlike the lights in the tent.

The longer she and Jack walked, the darker and quieter their surroundings grew. Trees that lined the drive soon obscured the house and tent from sight. By the time they reached the big oak tree, the music and light from the reception tent were replaced by the crunch of the gravel beneath their feet and the intermittent twinkling of lightning bugs in the meadow to the left of the driveway.

Reaching the oak tree, Jack lit a candle. Megan pulled the trigger on her automatic lighter and lit the candle across from Jack's. She walked eight to ten feet to the next jar and lit that one, and the next, and the next; Jack paralleled her, lighting candles on the opposite side of the path.

"I can't believe you pounded in all these stakes. There must be nearly a hundred of them," she said after lighting the tenth candle or so.

"Over a hundred." Jack released his trigger and moved on to the next one. "I didn't do it alone, though. The Latimer boys helped."

"But still . . . over a hundred?" Megan glanced back, admiring the soft glow of the candles lining the drive. "It looks really nice, if that's any consolation. But it's going to take us a while to finish."

Every thirty seconds or so they'd stop to light a candle. But talking along the way made the chore go faster.

"You don't mind, do you?" He didn't look at her.

"Mind what?"

"All of it. My folks, my family. They have a tendency to adopt people they like."

"Like Jeff Latimer and my brother, Eric?"

"Exactly. They kind of draw them into the family, sometimes against the victim's will."

"I don't think it's against anyone's will. Everyone in your family is so nice."

"Thanks, they like you too." Jack bent to light the last candle.

Megan had finished hers. She turned back to admire the long, double line of soft lights leading to the house. "Look how beautiful it is."

She glanced at Jack. This could have been a very romantic moment with the right man. Megan let the atmosphere soak in—the sparkling lights, the touching wedding, the entire evening that seemed to have a kind of dreamlike quality.

"Beautiful," he echoed, and she caught him staring at her.

Megan didn't care if she stood there all night with Jack. It was nice having him all to herself. Jack took her lighter from her, held her hand, and started back up the drive.

Aside from the few minutes spent in the flower garden this morning, they hadn't been alone since they arrived. Megan liked having Jack all to herself.

Taking their time, they strolled, very slowly, back to-ward the tent. They were nearing the big oak tree . . . halfway back. This had been their starting point. They were surrounded by candles leading away in both direc-tions on the driveway in the cool evening air. It still felt very . . . romantic to Megan, even with Jack.

They passed under the oak tree, and the closer they got to the tent, the slower they moved. Was she the one slowing down, or was she following Jack's diminishing pace? She wasn't sure. After a few more steps, she heard faint music.

Jack stopped. "Would you mind if we didn't go in right away?"

"No, I don't mind. It's nice out here." How did he know she didn't want to go back? She broke away from him, strolling to the other side of the drive. "We might miss the ceremonial first dance, though."

"I've seen Shelley and Jeff dance plenty of times. We're not missing anything." He crossed the drive and stood next to her.

It sounded as if *he* wanted to be alone with her too. Maybe thinking Jack wanted to kiss her wasn't entirely crazy.

She wanted him to hold her, wanted to feel his arms around her in more than a platonic way. He might never love her the way she wanted, but she could pretend he did, just for now, this one time.

Megan's shoulder brushed against him, and she smelled . . . "Is that rosemary?"

He lifted his boutonniere to his nose and inhaled. "Rose*Megan*—it will always remind me of you." His smile faded, and the expression in his eyes was the same as the previous night, when she'd thought he was going to kiss her.

What was happening? Some sort of wedding magic? His attention drifted from her eyes to her mouth and back. And it looked as if he was succumbing to the magic too.

Oh, yes, please . . . Let him do it, please. . . .

She lowered her eyelids and in half hope, half fear, willed him to do it.

This was an invitation for a kiss if ever he saw one, Jack decided.

Nothing would make him miss this precious moment with Megan. Not Shelley and Jeff's first dance, not a freak twister touching down, not a UFO crashing into the pony paddock. Nothing.

This was it. He had to make his move now. Jack took a steadying breath and prayed that he wasn't going to blow it. He was about to cross over the line of friendship; it was now or never, everything or nothing.

He leaned forward, feeling Megan warm and soft in his arms. *Perfect.* He lowered his head and pressed his lips to hers in a gentle kiss. She didn't pull back or try to slap him. What she did was return his kiss.

Nothing had ever felt so good in his life. He eased back just to catch his breath. He felt a little light-headed. He had done it, really done it. He'd kissed Megan. Was it his imagination, or had it been the most wonderful kiss ever?

"I love you," he whispered to her, hoping she'd be equally swept away by the twinkling lights and the romantic setting of the whole evening. That's what he was hoping for, anyway. But she said nothing.

He was so sure she'd wanted him to kiss her. Did she really feel nothing more for him than friendship? Was that the reason for her silence?

Jack leaned away from her. *Okay, they'd shared a moment, a kiss. But maybe that's all it was to her.*

Megan kept her eyes closed and stood as still as she could, savoring the kiss.

Oh, please, don't let this be a dream.

Jack had said something, but through the haze in her mind, she couldn't make out his words.

Had he said he was sorry? That he hadn't meant it? Megan didn't want to think about it. Not when she felt this bliss.

One minute the warmth of his breath caressed her cheek. The next, she was walking into the reception tent by his side. Megan couldn't remember what happened in between or how much time had passed. A minute? An hour?

They entered the tent amid the cheers and shrieks of bouncing girls and women. They must have been outside longer than she thought. How much of the reception had they missed? *What* had they missed?

Megan hardly had a chance to look around and get

her bearings when something came flying toward them and landed smack-dab in Jack's arms.

The bridal bouquet.

Jack stared from the flowers to Megan, clear shock on his face. The single, older females surrounding them groaned with disappointment.

"Look!" Jennifer yelled and pointed. "Uncle Jack's going to be the next bride!"

Chapter Twelve

Jack stood at the doorway of the reception tent holding Shelley's bridal bouquet. He passed the bouquet to Megan, who didn't have any choice but to hold it. "Here, I think this is meant for you."

The guests filed past them on their way out the door. Shelley and Jeff exited with well-wishing and cheers following them all the way to their chauffeured car. Shelley waved good-bye and stepped into the car. Jeff slid in beside her.

The limo moved down the candlelit drive as the guests waved and cheered the newlywed couple.

The voices subsided, and within a matter of minutes the guests began to dissipate. Some returned to the tent; some left.

"The party's over, kids." Eric stepped between Megan and Jack, draping his arms around their shoulders. "What a high! Why did I ever give this up?"

"*Vanity Fair*," Megan reminded him. "*Cosmo, GQ*— shall I go on?"

"They do tend to pay better, don't they?" He smiled.

"How about we find something to take care of my parched throat? I couldn't partake while I was on the job, but now that the festivities are over . . ."

Jack looked from Eric to Megan. He wanted to spend time with her, continue where they'd left off. Maybe convince her that the old wives' tale about the person who caught the bride's bouquet was true.

Whoa—hold on there! He was moving too fast.

"You two go ahead." Megan waved them away. "I have a post-reception, wind-down party to go to."

"What party? Why wasn't I invited?" Jack hadn't heard about any after-party party.

"It's for girls only. We're making popcorn and hot chocolate and putting our feet up."

"I think they're going to make you eat the leftover cereal," Eric joked.

As much as Jack wanted to be with Megan, maybe he should take some time to regroup.

"You're just hurt that you weren't invited. You and Eric haven't seen each other in a while. Why don't you two catch up?"

"Come on, Jackie, for old times' sake," Eric urged. "Or else your dad and those Latimer boys are going to make me lift something."

Jack asked Megan, "Are you sure you don't mind?"

She smiled. "Are you kidding? You'll see enough of me tomorrow. We're going to be stuck together for that five-hour flight home."

Oh, yeah. As if being "stuck together" would be something horrible.

"May I get a tall glass of sparkling water, please?" Eric leaned over the bar toward one of the bartenders who was busy packing up. "And if you can throw in a twist of lime, that would be great."

"I'll have whatever you've got available," Jack added.

The bartender slid a couple of glasses toward them and resumed his cleanup.

With his glass in hand, Eric collapsed into a chair. "I'd forgotten how hard these kinds of shoots are."

"After living through today, I can see how much pressure there is." Jack had never thought much about what his best friend had gone through during his early years as a photographer. "Running after the bride and groom, keeping pace with the momentum of the wedding."

"There's no retakes, you know. You get one shot only." Eric let out a sigh and took a deep drink.

"I guess we're not as young as we used to be." Jack took the chair next to Eric.

" 'We'? Speak for yourself, old man. *I'm* as young as I feel!" Eric quipped with an all-encompassing gesture. Then he kept particularly close watch on Jack when he asked, "Megan looked great, didn't she?"

That was an abrupt change of subject.

"Megan was beautiful," Jack replied, wondering where this was going.

"I think it's a good thing you kept an eye on her for

me when you moved out to California. You're like a substitute big brother."

"It never bothered to me to watch out for her. But it was *your* genius plan to drive her last few boyfriends away."

"Are you kidding? Those guys were creeps—none of them was good enough for her. You know that better than anyone." Eric leaned forward in his seat.

"Just because I agree with you doesn't mean you're right." Jack hadn't liked Eric's idea from the beginning, but he'd gone along with it. And if Megan ever learned what he'd done . . .

"So tell me, when was it you fell for her yourself?"

Jack choked, and he wasn't even drinking. "I . . . I . . . How did you—"

"It's amazing what one sees when one is behind a camera. It's almost as if I'm not even there. I can see it when you look at her. And she's just as crazy for you."

"What? Did she say something to you?"

"You'd have to be blind not to see it. She knows how you feel about her, right?"

"I told her I loved her tonight, and . . . I think it might have been a mistake."

"*Mistake?* You mean she didn't melt into a puddle at your feet?" Eric glanced heavenward and sighed in apparent disappointment.

"We kissed tonight." Why had he said that? Had Eric dumped some truth serum into his drink, or what?

"Your *first* kiss?" Eric straightened and kicked his feet off the chair next to him.

"If I've messed things up . . . there might not be any going back to being her friend." Jack didn't know what else to say.

"*Friends?* That's the *last* thing you want. Besides, like I said, she's crazy about you."

"Is she? *She* didn't mention that." Jack had expected more of a reaction from her when he told her he loved her. He'd wanted her to say that she felt the same, but apparently that wasn't what she felt at all.

"I bet you caught her off guard, didn't you? Meg wasn't expecting you to blurt that out. She didn't have time to react." Eric swung, slapping his friend on the arm with the back of his hand. "You've got to give her a chance to take it in, think about it. That's what girls do." Eric nodded knowingly and added, "Then you've got to make the big play."

"The 'big play'?" Jack wasn't entirely sure what his buddy was getting at.

"Come on, man, you've gotta make your move! Turn on the charm, *show* her what you mean. Don't be a wimp. She's on the high of watching a wedding; she's sentimental. Are you kidding? This is the perfect time to go for it!"

Megan carried a tray heaped with mugs for the hot chocolate into the front parlor. Ellen followed with a huge bowl of buttered popcorn and a plateful of oven-fresh cookies.

"Did you make that phone call to California?" Ellen asked.

"Yes, I left a message." Megan held the door open for Aunty Max, who brought up the rear carrying a pot of hot chocolate.

Jennifer picked up the bridal bouquet Megan had left on the coffee table.

"Don't touch the bouquet, Jenn. It belongs to Megan," Sarah scolded.

"Megan? Uncle Jack caught it," Brittney corrected her as big sisters did.

"Well, she's the one who's gonna get married next," Sarah fussed, unwilling to give in.

"Nuh-uh, Uncle Jack is," Brittney stated.

Aunty Max and Ellen set the cookies on the coffee table for everyone to help themselves.

"Who wants hot chocolate?" Megan passed out mugs to the raised hands before taking a seat next to Jennifer.

"I don't know how anyone could eat another bite." Aunty Max poured hot chocolate for the kids. "We ate enough at the reception to last us a week."

"Grandma, if Megan has the bride's bouquet, does that mean she's the next one to get married?" Jennifer asked, filling her bowl with popcorn.

"No," Brittney interrupted. "Uncle Jack caught the bouquet. That means he's the next one to get married." She took a chocolate chip cookie.

"I think Megan has to marry Uncle Jack," Sarah decided, and she sipped her hot chocolate. "Uncle Jack caught it and gave it to Megan. That means he *wants* to marry her. Don't you think so, Megan?"

Megan didn't know what to say.

"Hand me a bit of that popcorn, will you, Jenn?" Aunty Max passed her a small bowl to fill. "I don't want any salt. It's bad for my blood pressure."

"It's just an old wives' tale, girls," Ellen explained. "Catching the bridal bouquet really doesn't mean anything."

Thank goodness he doesn't have *to marry me.* Megan nodded, agreeing with their grandmother.

"It just gives us spinsters some hope," Aunty Max added.

Pamela came in from the hallway. "Billy's out like a light. Those ponies really wore him out. Remind me to thank Jack."

"Are you sure it wasn't all that dancing?" Aunty Max motioned for Brittney and Sarah to make a spot for their mother between them. "I don't think he sat one out."

"I *loved* riding the ponies!" Jennifer clasped her hands in front of her, looked heavenward, and held her breath.

"Let's all talk about our favorite part of the day," Brittney suggested. "Mine was everyone watching me walk down the aisle in my beautiful gown and holding the flowers."

"It was a dress, not a gown," Sarah corrected.

"What-*ever*!"

"What was your favorite part, Mom?" Jennifer asked around a mouthful of food.

"I don't know." Pamela balanced her elbows on her

knees and rubbed her chin, giving the question some thought. "I like it when the whole family gets together."

Aunty Max wrapped her arm around Sarah. "I thought Andy Latimer was a dead man for tying Shelley's wedding ring to the satin pillow."

"He would have been if Billy had lost her ring." The look in Pamela's eyes told Megan she'd meant every word.

Kissing Jack had been Megan's favorite part, but she couldn't talk about that in front of his family.

After spending the next hour talking about the wedding and identifying their favorite parts, Megan began to wonder if she and Jack had really kissed or if she had imagined it.

She couldn't stop thinking about it . . . him . . . she couldn't think straight. Real or imagined, she hadn't forgotten how it felt. She touched her lips with her fingers, recalling the moment.

Dreamy, delicious, delightful.

She'd never wanted to kiss anyone that much in her whole life.

But it didn't matter. Their kiss couldn't have meant as much to him as it had to her. Of that much Megan was certain.

Chapter Thirteen

Megan and Jack hadn't returned home as a couple the way he had thought they would. Not only had Jack wasted the whole trip home, he'd wasted the entire four days alone with her. Correction: "alone time" with Megan had never happened.

Eric was right: Jack had to do something. He needed to somehow recreate the "wedding magic" they'd felt . . . but without the wedding. He had to make his move before Megan and her Mr. Right got back together. And it would have to be something special and romantic.

A candlelit dinner at his place, some music, and then after they'd both have a glass of wine. While reminiscing over the last few days, he'd tell her about his feelings. Then he'd pull out a diamond engagement ring and ask her to marry him right there on the spot. No more delays, no more putting anything off. He had to do it.

He'd make all his plans for the romantic evening tomorrow at work. Tonight they'd settle into their old routine, make her feel safe and secure before he turned on the charm tomorrow night.

Megan stepped into her apartment, leaned back

against the door, and closed her eyes. The familiar yet unreal feeling of being home washed over her. Here was life as usual, but could she go back to anything normal?

After this trip, she was more in love with Jack than ever. She'd started out by doing him a favor, and now that favor was ruining her life. Trying to fall in love with another man had been difficult before the trip; now it might be impossible.

All that cozy togetherness Megan had felt with Jack these last few days wasn't real. None of it. No matter how perfect it had felt at the time.

Jack could only be her very good, dear friend, and that's all. She had to get over it. Get over him.

Blinking away the tears pooling in her eyes, Megan could make out the fuzzy, flashing, red message light on her answering machine. She set her bags on the floor, headed for the counter, and pushed the PLAY button.

"You have three new messages," the answering machine said. "Message one. Friday, 8:59 A.M."

"Hi, Megan, it's Leslie. I know you're not back yet, but I just wanted to say hi and welcome home. I hope you had a wonderful trip. Can't wait to hear about it on Monday. See you then."

Wonderful? That was a joke. *Horrible, terrible* was the way Megan would describe it. *Awful.* She inhaled, holding the heavy, sinking feeling inside, doing her best not to cry.

"Message two," said the monotoned digital voice of the recorder. "Saturday, 1:28 P.M."

"Hi, it's me."

Brandon.

"I'm on a layover in Austin, and I just had to call to tell you how much I miss you."

During his brief pauses Megan could hear the jumble of voices and the bustling sounds of the airport in the background.

"I can't wait until I see you on Monday. Just can't wait. See ya, babe. Bye."

He wanted to be with her, wanted her. Megan could hear it in his voice. Could she make it work with Brandon? Could she learn to love him? Everything would be so easy if she could just be in love with him.

"Message three. Saturday, 10:12 P.M."

"Yes, I'm calling myself."

Megan was startled at the sound of her own voice on the machine. She'd forgotten she'd left a message for herself. She'd even forgotten what it was about.

"I just wanted to give myself a reality check when I get back home. Jack may have seemed all warm and cozy, and he is, but not the way you think." Her voice was also a monotone, and Megan remembered how she'd tried to keep from crying as she spoke. "He's a great guy, a great friend, and you've done him a favor. And I knew before the trip ever started that this might have been a bad idea. I just want to remind myself not to read any more into what happened between us than—" She'd broken off as her throat closed up with emotion. "I just wanted to remind myself that I'm very, very lucky to have him as a friend. Because he's a good one."

Reality check. Megan leaned against the counter, rubbing her eyes.

"End of messages," the voice said.

That's okay. Megan got it, loud and clear.

Jack paid the pizza delivery boy and headed over to Megan's. He knocked on her door before letting himself in. "You all unpacked yet?"

Megan looked up from the kitchen counter. "Unpacked? My luggage is still sitting in the living room."

Sure enough, there were her bags, sitting right at the end of the sofa. Megan's eyes were narrowed; she looked as if she'd been crying or on the verge. "What's the matter?"

"Tired, I guess." She rubbed her forehead, looking fatigued and in need of a good night's sleep. "Jet lag, you know, the whole traveling bit."

Jack slid the pizza box onto the table and nodded. Yeah, he knew.

"You brought food? I thought you weren't feeling well during the flight home. How can you possibly think of food after—"

"That was then. This is now." He pulled a couple of plates from the cabinet. "Go have a seat and get comfy. We can watch something on the Explorer Channel."

There really wasn't an Explorer Channel. That was their shorthand for several cable stations they frequented that had all sorts of humans-versus-wild-animals-in-remote-areas types of shows; *Survivor Man, Man v. Wild,* and *Surviving the Wild* were among their favorites.

Megan sat. She must have been tired. She was staring at the blank TV and said nothing.

He flipped on the set before handing her a plate and a soda. He settled next to her on the sofa. "Isn't this great? Just like the good old days." He popped the top on his ginger ale with a fizz.

"Yeah." She smiled and bit into the pizza. "Just like the good old days."

How lucky could she get? They'd chanced on to a *Surviving the Wild* marathon. A half hour later, Jack was still sitting there beside her, and he'd be there for . . . how much longer? The whole marathon?

They watched one episode after another featuring a brave or crazy Aussie, Blake Armstrong, in the desert, in the jungle, and on mountaintops. He traveled to different continents of the world, handling snakes, spiders, and all sorts of reptiles.

During a commercial break between episodes, Jack announced, "I'm ready for some ice cream. How about you?"

"Ice cream? How could you?" Megan protested. Jack had managed to eat four slices of pizza. After her two pieces it seemed that the jet lag Megan had felt just an hour before disappeared. Either she could attribute that to jumping with fright at every strike of the king cobra Blake avoided, or she was thoroughly enjoying her personal Jack-fest. She couldn't decide which.

"By jingo, I'm definitely ready for ice cream. How

about you, mate?" Jack decided in his best Aussie accent.

Megan shrugged.

Jack leaped out of his seat the way Blake leaped away from a striking poisonous snake. "Blimey, I didn't bring any ice cream."

"I don't think that's a problem, Jack-o."

"We'll have to seek out the ice cream's lair and see if we can scare some up."

Jack was so silly. She watched him carefully make his way from the sofa to the kitchen, checking for attacking creatures at every turn.

"You gotta keep a-lart. No telling what snake might slither up behind you and bite!" He mimicked a snake striking with his hand.

"Gee, I never realized the trip to the kitchen was so hazardous."

"It's dodgy, I tell ya!" Jack wiped off imaginary sweat from his brow when he made it to the refrigerator in one piece. He pulled open the freezer door and didn't have to peer too far inside. "Did you know you have a zillion tubs of ice cream in here?"

"Tell me about it. You're the one who brought them over."

"Not all these." He stared at the group of cartons.

"Well, maybe not *all* of them." It wasn't as if Megan kept track of what Jack brought when, but she knew she hadn't bought more than one or two varieties of ice cream. She rolled to her knees and faced him. "You do bring a new one almost every night."

"I do?"

"We never finish them, so they just pile up."

Jack looked deeper into the freezer, apparently trying to see all the way to the back. "I think they might be multiplying on their own. All right-y, let's do something about it." He started pulling out pint containers. "We've got some Tin Roof Sundae; an all-time favorite, Cookies 'n' Cream. . . ." He set them on the counter next to the fridge. "Here's . . . oh, this sounds good . . . triple Caramel Crunch. This one's plain ole strawberry, and here's . . . Chunky Monkey? Strange . . ." He held the container up and glanced off to one side. "I don't remember ever buying this one."

Megan had to admit, that was one she'd bought during one of her low "dating" moments. "You're not going to eat all of those tonight, are you?"

"We don't have to eat all of them. I just want to know what my choices are. We'll clean out the freezer and neaten things up a bit."

He set the Chunky Monkey down with the rest of the containers. "Aw . . .'ave a look at this. This one's a beauty—chocolate chocolate chip, and here's another strawberry. Is strawberry a favorite of someone's?"

"It's not a crime to like strawberry."

Jack had placed the half dozen or so pints on a large plate and made it back to his seat on the sofa beside her just as the next episode of *Surviving the Wild* started.

"Why do you have *two* brands of strawberry?" Jack gripped one spoon and held out a second one for Megan.

"They're different. I mean, they taste different."

He gave her an are-you-sure-you-know-what-you're-talking-about look.

"It depends what I'm in the mood for," she explained. But it didn't look as if it was doing any good. "You're not planning for us to eat this right out of the cartons, are you? That's barbaric."

"Sure. Why not?" He shrugged. "We're among friends; let's live dangerously." Jack picked up a pint container. "You don't mean to tell me you think there's a difference between these strawberries?"

"You don't know? I thought you were an ice cream connoisseur." Because Jack was selective about the kind of ice cream he ate, Megan thought that meant he truly *knew* his ice creams.

He placed a spoonful of strawberry into his mouth. "For an ice cream that doesn't have chocolate or caramel, it's pretty good. Now for the competitor." He sampled the other one. "About the same. It's ice cream."

"The same? How can you say it's the same? They're both the same flavor, but they don't *taste* the same."

"Don't tell me you can *really* tell a difference between the two. No way."

"Yes, way. I'll prove it." Megan clapped her hands over her eyes. "I promise I won't peek." She dropped her mouth open, parting her lips, waiting for the first spoonful.

The ice cream almost melted completely in the carton Jack held, proof of the instantaneous temperature spike. He spooned a bit of it and raised it toward her mouth.

He stopped. His gazed fixed on her lips . . . her beautiful, inviting lips. Lowering the spoon, he leaned closer, bringing his lips nearer to hers, and let his eyes slide shut.

No, not yet. He shouldn't. He had to wait for the right moment. Jack lifted the spoonful of strawberry ice cream soup and said, "Open wide."

The right moment would be tomorrow night.

Get over it. Get over him, Megan told herself early that Monday morning all the way during her commute on the bus. She'd been repeating it ever since Jack left her place last night.

Dinner was nice, and Jack was sweet as always. And everything was exactly the way it had been before they left. Nothing had changed, which proved she was right. She had no romantic future with Jack. It was going to be hard to wean herself off him.

Get over it. Get over him, she reminded herself.

Leslie plopped down at her desk and dropped her purse into the bottom drawer, pushing it closed with her foot. "You don't look so good, Megan."

"That's an understatement. I feel like—" Megan sank into her chair and rested her elbows on her desk, burying her face in her hands.

"Don't tell me something *did* happen between you

and Jack." Leslie wheeled her chair closer to Megan, showing interest. "Well, let's hear it."

"Jack's sister's wedding"—Megan paused, then proceeded cautiously—"was great."

"And? What about you and Jack?"

"He . . . kissed me."

"Finally!" Leslie gasped, her eyes wide with amazement.

"Yeah." Megan felt embarrassed by the confession. It sounded like more than what had really happened—because nothing *had* really happened.

"And what did you do?"

Megan shrugged. "I kissed him back."

"Darn tootin' you did. You're not crazy, you know. You're just like any other red-blooded American girl. So, did you talk about it? This *thing* between you?"

"We got back yesterday, and Jack and I spent last night—" Megan paused, not sure exactly how to phrase it without sounding totally lame. "Last night we just had pizza and watched *Surviving the Wild.* We were in luck—they were running a marathon." Megan shrugged. "Same ol', same ol'." She stood and walked to Leslie's desk. What Megan wanted to do was bang her head against a wall.

"So, he's . . . thinking? Feeling? What?"

"I don't know. I don't think anything's changed for him." Megan felt herself getting choked up and didn't want to cry. "I've got to do something, Les. This can't go on. I'm afraid I'm really falling in love with him but . . . I can't have him." Megan paced back and forth and forth and back. "I'm going to drive myself crazy."

" 'Falling'?" Clearly Leslie was about to let her have it whether Megan wanted to hear it or not. "You've jumped headfirst into the Jack chasm without a parachute is more like it—without a net, to boot."

"I know. I have to get over him." Megan felt totally sorry for herself. "If I don't do something about my love life now, I'll never have one."

"A love life?"

Megan nodded. "A husband, a family, any of that. The wedding I just went to made me realize that Jack will always be there for me, but not in the way I want."

"That sounds cold."

"That's reality." Megan sat on the edge of Leslie's desk. "Brandon Wright left me a message while I was gone. I know he's interested in me, and I want to be interested in him too. I could be, I'm sure."

"You can't *make* yourself love him."

Whose side was Leslie on, anyway?

"No, but now I know that nothing more is ever going to happen with Jack. I think that Brandon may truly be thinking about a wife, a family, a future. That's what I want, and he might be just the guy. I've got to give him a chance. And I need to give myself a chance to fall in love with him."

Chapter Fourteen

At 9:00 A.M. Jack strolled through the lobby of Tri-Logic and headed for his office. He had done exactly what he'd wanted last night—put himself back at square one and made sure he hadn't lost any ground. Tonight he'd make his big move.

"There he is! Hail Caesar, back from the campaign! Alexander, returning from his march!" Richard chanted, following Jack down the hall. "No . . . you're Bill Gates with his triumphant announcement of Windows at COMDEX!"

"You're quoting ancient history." Jack set his brief-case on his desk and sat, trying his best to ignore Richard, but the man wasn't going away.

"Uh-oh, what happened?" Richard leaned against the doorway.

Jack sent a dark glare Richard's way.

"Struck out again, I see," Richard commented.

Jack had not "struck out"; he hadn't even gotten up to bat yet. "Just go back to work, will you?"

Richard backed down and went slinking off to his

cubicle, but not before Jack caught his departing smirk and a muffled evil chuckle.

Jack didn't have any time to waste as he pulled out the notes and tentative list he'd made for his plans tonight.

His big play.

Food, flowers, and the most important item: Vanda's Jewelers for the ring. He'd call after ten and speak to Vanda personally.

Jack had strolled by the jewelry store more than a couple times. He'd gazed in the front window, dreaming of what kind of engagement ring Megan might want. Vanda had invited him in, and they'd had some lengthy conversations about diamonds. Today Jack would take one step further and actually make the purchase. Something simple but impressive.

After buying the ring, he'd go home, start dinner, create a romantic atmosphere, and wait for Megan to return—then he'd surprise her.

The phone rang. Jack answered, "This is Jack." He wedged the receiver between his ear and shoulder.

"And I'm delighted!" the caller replied. "How's my future brother-in-law to-be?"

"Hi, Eric." Jack relaxed and took hold of the phone receiver.

"What's up? Shall I pencil in another wedding shoot?"

Jack could hear his best friend's obvious wink through the phone line. "No."

"No? What the heck have you been doing? You had all yesterday *and* all last night."

Eric had a way of making Jack's situation sound even worse than it was. A lot worse. "I really haven't pressed the issue yet."

"You're talking about being in love, not hitting up venture capitalists for funding." There was a pause. "You've got to make your move—now, before it's too late. You're coming off the high of a wedding. You've got the whole wedding bells, honeymoon, throwing-rice thing going for you."

"Puffed rice," Jack corrected.

"Whatever . . . you know what I'm talking about. The point is, you can't let things cool down between you two. You've swept her off her feet; don't let her fall. You've got to catch her before someone else comes along and snags her."

"Brandon." He spit out the name.

"What did you say?"

"Brandon Wright. That's the guy she's seeing now."

"You've successfully gotten rid of guys before."

"I'm not proud of that, Eric."

"Yeah, but this time you'd be doing it for yourself."

Jack glanced at his watch. It was nearing eleven. "I've got to go. I've got to make plans to pick up her engagement ring."

"Good! You the man—remember that." And then Eric Donnelly hung up.

Jack leaped out of his chair and ran down the hall. He had two hours to see the people he had to see and finish up at work before his appointment at the jeweler. On his way there, he'd stop by Megan's office and invite her to his place for dinner.

He had to remember that he *was* the man, not Brandon Wright. All that was left was to prove it.

Jack walked into Megan's office—Papers, Pens, and Pencils—and glanced around. The receptionist's desk stood empty. A ding from the elevator down the hall caught his attention. Out of the corner of his eye, he glimpsed none other than Brandon Wright heading his way. Although Jack knew who Brandon was, Brandon had never laid eyes on him.

Think fast. It's not that Jack was intentionally interfering in Megan's life . . . he just wanted to put up a roadblock or two.

Jack ran around the desk, donned the headset, and pressed a few phone line buttons, making himself look busy, as if he belonged there and knew what he was doing. Brandon dropped his business card in front of Jack and waited.

"May I help you?" Jack said, sitting ramrod straight and over-enunciating each word.

"I'm here to see Megan Donnelly."

"And who may I say is calling?" Jack widened his eyes in pseudo interest and raised his eyebrows.

"Brandon Wright."

"And you represent whom?" Jack turned an ear toward the salesman as if he were truly paying attention.

Brandon hammered the business card with his index finger. "Allied Federated."

"Oh," Jack said in an almost disappointed sigh and looked at the card in front of him. "Right," he said in a dropped tone, inferring finality. "I see." He lifted the card and held it directly in front of his face. Peeking over the top of the card, he said, "And I should tell Ms. Donnelly that your visit would be concerning . . . ?"

"It's personal," Brandon said in the most hostile tone Jack could imagine. *Good.* This guy was close to blowing his stack. Maybe he had some anger issues.

Jack held back a smile and openly eyed Brandon from his stylishly cut hair, past his tailored suit, to his shiny black oxfords. "I'll tell her you're here," he said as if he was doing this guy a favor. He pushed a button and spoke into his headset. "Ms. Donnelly? There's a Mr. Wright here to see you."

Brandon rubbed his jaw and shifted his weight from one foot to the other. Anxious, was he? Jack was going to do what he could to make Brandon totally lose his cool.

Glancing up, Jack pretended he was on the receiving end of a conversation with Megan. "All right. Yes. I'll tell him." He pressed a button, terminating the nonexistent connection.

"She's asked me to tell you she has a meeting that's just come up and that she'll be in touch with you." Jack glanced around, guaranteeing their privacy, and leaned forward. "Between you and me," he said in a confidential whisper, "sounds like a brush-off." Brandon wasn't asking, but Jack was going to tell him anyway.

Wright narrowed his eyes. "You think so?"

"Definitely," Jack responded with a decisive nod, giving his receptionist performance all the sincerity he could muster.

"I'll just give her a call at *home* later," Brandon replied smartly, sounding impatient and on edge. Then he left.

The way he'd emphasized *home* made it sound as if he had some secret "in" with Megan. He didn't know Jack already knew his history. Brandon might think he was going to call Megan at *home*—but *later* was going to be too late for Mr. Not Right.

Jack watched Brandon disappear into the elevator. He tapped the eraser end of a pencil on the desk.

There was something off about that guy.

Jack still didn't know what it was. But it didn't matter. Brandon Wright wasn't going to be around long enough for it to matter.

Ten minutes later, Jack stepped into Megan's office.

"Jack, what are you doing here?" Megan pushed a filing-cabinet drawer closed.

"You're not happy to see me?"

"Of course. But I was expecting—"

"Who?"

"Brandon."

"Who?" Jack repeated an octave higher.

"You know, Brandon."

Jack snapped his fingers. "Oh, yeah, 'Mr. Right.' How could I have forgotten?"

Megan checked her watch. "It's already twelve-thirty. Something must have come up."

"It happens." Jack shrugged.

"But he sounded so eager to see me. I thought he was, anyway."

Maybe Jack was wrong about her feelings for Wright. Maybe she was truly interested in Brandon and really upset that he hadn't shown.

"What *are* you doing here, Jack?"

"Me?" He felt like an idiot. "Oh, uh . . . I . . . I was just running an errand out this way. I thought I'd stop by."

"Since it looks like I've been stood up and you're here, how about you take me to lunch?"

That was an improvement. She'd asked him, but she didn't sound all that happy about the change in her plans.

Megan sat in her office after lunch. Being with Jack was never a disappointment, but being with him wasn't what she needed. She needed to be *away* from him, to find a man of her own. It didn't help that she'd also made plans to have dinner with him after work.

Leslie hadn't returned from lunch yet, and Megan got to sit there all by her lonesome and think about spending another evening alone with Jack. It wasn't what she needed.

The phone rang. "Papers, Pencils, and Pens, Megan Donnelly."

"Hello, Megan Donnelly."

"Brandon? What happened? You should have called if you got held up."

"Called? I came by, and your receptionist told me *you* had a meeting. I even got a little enlightened advice—that you were dumping me."

"Dumping you?" That didn't sound right. Gina would never have said anything like that. "That's crazy. I'm not dumping you."

"I thought something strange was going on. It doesn't matter now. What matters is that we find some time to get back together. I really missed you."

He was right. Megan wanted—no, *needed*—time with him as soon as possible.

"I hate to give you bad news, but I've got this off-site meeting coming up. It's supposed to be within the next week or two; actually, it could happen any time now. I don't know when I'll be called away or when I'll be back, and I really want to see you. We need to make the most of the time we have."

He was right; they had already been apart for too long. "What did you have in mind?"

"You, me, a pastrami poor boy, and a Sam Adams Pale Ale."

"Sounds good. My place at seven?" She might be pushing it by inviting him to her apartment, but she had to get things moving and get Jack out of her system.

"I can't wait that long. Make it six." He sounded eager, and not particularly for that po'boy he'd mentioned.

Megan was going for it. "You bring the sandwich, and I'll pick up the beer."

The six-pack Megan had picked up after work was cooling in the refrigerator. She hadn't realized until she got home that she had forgotten to call Jack and cancel their dinner plans, but it didn't really matter. She knew he'd understand. She'd give him a buzz right after she finished dressing.

She agonized over what to wear for her big evening. Nothing slinky or obvious as Leslie had suggested. Megan ended up donning a burgundy long-sleeved chenille sweater that cried "touch me" and black slacks. She brushed her hair smooth and silky to blend in with the whole take-me-in-your-arms-and-hold-me look.

Megan called Jack's office. He'd left for the day. Then she tried his cell. He didn't answer. She'd have to try again later.

Stepping into the living room, she did her best to re-create the same kind of atmosphere she'd seen in the movies: soft lights, breezy music, and lots of candles to create the perfect romantic scene.

After grouping candles of various sizes and shapes

on the coffee table and bookcase against the wall in the living room, she stepped back to admire the effect. She liked it. It was perfect. Just perfect.

She had to hurry; Brandon would be here any minute. Megan set the table, putting out a couple of plates and cloth napkins.

This had to work. Had to.

In his apartment, Jack dimmed the room lights just enough to make sure the focus of attention went to the glow of the candles on the dining table. He smoothed the crisp white linen tablecloth and adjusted the creases of the folded napkins on the two place settings so they sat just so.

He'd make one last check across the room before heading over to Megan's to escort her here for the most romantic evening of her life.

The china plates, silverware, and glasses were all in place. The Champagne flutes were chilling in the refrigerator along with the bottle of blanc de blanc Champagne, waiting for the celebratory moment when it would be time to pop the cork.

One hit on the PLAY button of his CD player and Pavarotti began his serenade. Assured that everything was perfect, Jack stepped out his front door and headed down the hall.

He stopped outside Megan's door and checked for the small velvet box in his pocket. He rapped on the door before walking in.

"Hey, Meg, are you ready to—" Jack's eyes widened. Talk about some enchanted evening. . . . The music, the candles, the lighting . . . her apartment looked a lot like—like . . . his. Jack swallowed hard. He didn't like the déjà vu feeling creeping up his spine. "Is that Sinatra singing 'Strangers in the Night'?"

"Jack . . ." Megan spun to face him. "I sorry. I tried to call you to cancel tonight."

"Are you expecting company?" Jack hated to think all this effort was for . . . "Mr. Right?" But he could tell by the way she was dressed.

"I'm sorry. You don't mind, do you? You said tonight would just be us getting together, just a regular evening." She ran her hands up and down her sleeves, looking very self-conscious. "Brandon and I are going to catch up on lost time."

Catch up? With the low lights and the romantic music wafting through her apartment, it didn't look as if she'd planned for an evening of casual conversation.

"You're not mad, are you, Jack?"

Yes, but he couldn't say anything about it. "That's what I said, all right—nothing special." He shrugged as if it hadn't meant anything to him. Jack shouldn't have made their evening sound so casual. Tonight was supposed to be the most important night of their lives.

Megan stepped to the bookcase and fiddled with the candles, grouping and regrouping them. "So if you don't mind . . ."

She wanted him to leave. "You got it," he answered.

Megan was cool toward him, and he hated it. He was angry with himself for being bested by Brandon. "I'll make myself scarce. When are you expecting him?"

"At six."

"Well, then, I'll be out of your hair in a jiff." Jack strolled to the fridge to help himself to a ginger ale before vacating the premises.

All he'd need was for Brandon to catch a glimpse of him; a casual meeting in the hallway would do. Jack wouldn't be the only one with a ruined evening.

Opening the fridge, he spotted six bottles of alien amber ale. Those didn't belong there. Brandon was an intruder—first his woman, now his fridge space.

Jack glanced at Megan, still busy with the candles on the coffee table. He pulled out the nearest bottle of beer, gave it a couple of good, vigorous shakes, and replaced it on the shelf.

Being sprayed with beer could make anyone lose their cool. He didn't care that he had to resort to a childish prank. He was desperate.

"No, come on, really." She marched into the kitchen and pulled Jack out by the arm. "You've got to go. He'll be here any minute."

Jack made the motion of checking his watch. "He's late by my calculations."

"What?" Megan grabbed Jack's wrist to look at his watch.

"Ouch, ouch, ouch."

"Five after?"

The dejected look in her eyes made Jack hesitate. He hated to see her hurting, even if it was over this jerk. Was Brandon Wright really that important to her? Jack didn't want to think so.

Something was wrong; Megan knew it. Even with her sweater on, she felt chills run up her arms. "Wait, please don't go, Jack. Will you stay while I call him?"

"You really want me to stick around?"

"Moral support." She forced a smile, then picked up her cordless phone and a business card from the kitchen counter.

Jack eased into the sofa. "I'm here for you. Mr. Moral Support."

Megan scanned Brandon's card and punched in his number. It rang once, and a computerized voice said, "Your call is being forwarded."

Then a woman answered, "Allied Federated, this is the 24/7 on-call line."

"I'm trying to get hold of Brandon Wright. This is his cell number, right?" Megan glanced at Jack, feeling the butterflies taking flight in her stomach while she waited for her answer.

"Just a moment, let me check his status." Silence for several seconds. The woman came back. "I'm sorry, Mr. Wright is listed as on an extended leave."

"Excuse me?" Megan must have heard incorrectly. "What kind of leave?"

"Paternity leave."

"What? Are you . . . are you sure?" Megan knew

there must have been some sort of mistake. The woman couldn't have been talking about her Brandon. "I'm calling for Brandon Wright. Brandon. *W-R-I-G-H-T.*"

"Let me double-check, ma'am." Silence on the line again. "From what this says, he was put on leave when his wife went into labor this afternoon."

His wife?

Labor?

He's married. And about to be a father too.

It was sinking in, but Megan was too numb to feel anything.

Mr. Right was married and expecting a baby. She couldn't believe it.

Could not believe it.

"Is there someone else who can help you, ma'am? Ma'am?"

"What?"

"Would you like to leave a message?" When Megan didn't answer, the woman said, "If this is an emergency, I could direct your call elsewhere."

What could she say? Megan barely got out a no and lowered the phone receiver from her ear.

"What is it?" Jack was at her side in an instant and helped her sit on the sofa.

How could she be so wrong about a person? She had the absolute worst luck with men.

Jack perched on the sofa. "What's happened?"

Megan looked Jack straight in the eye and said, "Brandon is married."

"Married?" Jack knew it, he knew it! He'd known there was something that screamed *all wrong* about that guy.

"And his wife is having a baby."

"A baby?" This was better than Jack could have ever imagined. "What an A-one pig. How could he do this to you? How could he—"

"It must be me." Megan leaned into couch and dropped her head back.

"What do you mean you?"

"I sure know how to pick them, don't I?"

"Look, Meg, you've got to trust me on this. It's not your fault. Mr. Wright has always been Mr. Wrong for you." Jack pulled her to him, wrapping his arms around her. She cuddled against his chest.

He felt a twinge of guilt about holding her close. He was supposed to be comforting her, not enjoying himself, but he couldn't help it.

"That's it." Megan pushed away from Jack and stood. "I'm through with men."

Chapter Fifteen

"What?"

"I never, ever want anything to do with another man as long as I live." She crossed her heart and hoped to die if she broke her vow.

This wasn't the way this was supposed to turn out. "Come on, don't you think you're overreacting?"

"Overreacting?" Megan swiped at her tears of anger. "I've got the worst record for men. They're slobs or users or indifferent or *married*. No more, Jack. I can't do this anymore."

She couldn't mean that. Not now.

"You're not being fair," he pleaded with her.

She could not do this. Jack had never gotten his chance with her, to prove that all the men of the world weren't as horrible as she thought.

"What do you care?" she snapped.

"I care . . . a lot." His words came out stiffly.

This wasn't the way he'd pictured telling her. There was supposed to be Pavarotti playing in the background, not Sinatra. He was supposed to work up to telling her he had more than friendly feelings for her, not blurt them out while they were in a heated discussion.

"Why would you care if I dated another man or not?" She faced him.

"I care," he said. "I care because . . ." What he had planned didn't matter anymore. *This was it.* Jack had to say it. He swallowed hard. He was about to cross the line. "I care because *I'm* interested."

"*You're* interested . . . in *me*?" Megan inched back, confusion clouding her face.

"I already told you how I felt . . . right after we kissed." Hadn't she heard him tell her he loved her? "I thought it would make a difference."

"What? I didn't . . . I don't remember. I didn't hear you." She whispered in disbelief, "I never thought you were interested in me."

How could she not know? Jack wondered. Hadn't he always been there for her? He kept her company, brought her Chinese food, did her laundry when she couldn't handle the stairs, and, as difficult as it was, he'd always been a shoulder to cry on, someone she could turn to when the latest new ex-boyfriend had let her down.

"I thought you always thought of me as Eric's kid sister, and somehow you couldn't . . . Maybe you felt you'd be betraying him by getting . . . involved with me."

"You thought all those things?" Jack never imagined his confession would be met with a list of excuses.

Jack stalked to the fridge, opened the door, decided

against the ginger ale, and went for the beer instead. He twisted off the cap, and the contents sprayed all over him and across the kitchen. Jack stood perfectly still.

"Okay," he said, very controlled while the beer dripped off the end of his nose. "I think I'd better go home."

Jack headed out of Megan's apartment and back to his own to clean up and cool down.

That's right. Get out and stay out. Megan pushed the door shut behind Jack with her foot. *Good riddance.* Why was *he* angry, anyway?

Megan punched the room lights on, strode to the stereo, and flipped off Sinatra. She slapped out the flames of the row of candles sitting on the bookcase.

Why had Jack waited so long to say something to her?

He'd had plenty of chances—at the wedding or the rehearsal dinner or the five-hour plane ride either to or from home.

Megan sank into the sofa, then leaned forward to pinch out the flames of the candles on the coffee table. She watched the tendrils of smoke climb, climb, climb to the ceiling.

How about after they'd kissed? *That* seemed like the perfect time. Why hadn't he told her then?

Oh . . . he'd said he did. Jack told her he *had* said something. Megan still didn't know what that *something* was.

So maybe some of this was her fault. And maybe she

shouldn't have snapped at him. Okay, *maybe* she owed him an apology. Megan headed for Jack's.

Not more than twenty minutes had passed when she knocked on his door three times, hard.

"Come in!"

Megan stepped inside, ready to demand he speak to her, but she froze where she stood.

A soul-felt opera aria crooned by a tenor played softly in the background.

The side-by-side settings at the dining table had been set in accordance to Emily Vanderbilt or Martha Stewart's high standards. The beautiful floral centerpiece had a least a half dozen candles.

"What's going on in here?" she asked cautiously.

Jack stood at the sink with a pile of dishes stacked next to him on the counter. He worked vigorously, scrubbing them in the sink.

"I'm washing the dishes," he said into the kitchen sink. He wore an apron tied at his waist and neck.

"Don't you have a dishwasher?" Megan still couldn't quite figure out what was going on.

"I'm not washing them because they're dirty. I'm washing them because I'm angry."

"You're washing clean dishes?" Megan looked around, noting the immaculate condition of his apartment. "If you always clean when you're mad, you must really have a temper."

Jack turned, leaned against the counter, and just looked at her. Without a word, he pulled the dishtowel from his shoulder with a rubber-gloved hand and wiped the plate dry.

"It's better than being on the lookout for girlfriends I don't want."

"Come on, you can do better than that. Guys are always on the lookout for women."

"I'm not like Kevin." Jack placed the dry plate in a cupboard and crossed his arms.

"Kevin?" Megan had told Jack only what she wanted him to know about Kevin. Which wasn't much. She had passed on an edited version of what really happened.

"That guy was quite the Romeo. He would have added you to his conquest list if you hadn't seen him hit on the blond bombshell."

Megan had caught Kevin with his hands full of blond ambition on her return to their table after a trip to the powder room. Megan had broken up with him on the spot.

All she had said to Jack was that she'd had it with the jerk's checking out other women while they were out for dinner.

"I never told anyone about that." Megan had been too embarrassed to tell anyone the slimy details.

Jack pulled off his rubber gloves and set them on the counter. "I know because"—he untied his apron and slipped it over his head—"I set it up."

"What?" Megan stood there for a few seconds, unable to speak. What was he talking about? How could he have done that? Why did he do it? *No.* "You did . . . what?"

Megan ripped the apron out of Jack's hands. Instead of strangling him with it, she threw it to the floor. "What right do you have to interfere in my life?" He didn't have any, as far as she was concerned.

"He was a creep, and you weren't picking up on the signals. So I *helped* you see them."

" 'Helped'?" She couldn't believe it. "Did you 'help' me with any of my other boyfriends?"

"Well . . ." His voice grew quiet. "Eric wasn't here to protect you, so he thought I could. . . . It was a stupid idea."

"How many, Jack?" Megan was sure she wasn't going to like the answer. "How many?" she repeated, insisting he answer.

"There was Jerry. . . ." he began.

Jerry was a total loser. Megan didn't know why she'd ever fallen for him. She must have been desperate.

"And then there was Andrew, the sports fan."

Megan had nearly forgotten about him. If there was any timed event involving a ball and boundary lines, it was an occasion that would capture Andrew's attention.

"I didn't know he was a sports nut until I saw him watching a basketball game . . . then a hockey game . . . then a boxing match . . . then a football game . . . on TV. I got the idea of sending him tickets, to any kind of sports games, to lure him away from you."

"You did that?"

"He wasn't good enough for you. None of them were. I was just trying to help you see their defects."

Megan had never seen this side of Jack before. After all the time they'd spent together, may be she didn't really know him at all.

"I hated seeing you with those guys, Meg."

Megan couldn't believe it. He was all those things the others were: self-centered, manipulating, and controlling.

Megan rubbed her eyes. She felt tired, drained.

Confusion, astonishment, and betrayal rushed through her in an uncontrollable surge. "I've told you everything—*everything.*" Just as she would a girlfriend. But he wasn't just like a girlfriend. He was a guy, who apparently was interested in her.

How could Jack have done this to her? Megan had trusted him, confided in him. And he'd betrayed her. Hurt and betrayed her. Totally.

"Isn't that great?" Smiling, Jack stepped closer, running his hands up and down her arms. It made her uncomfortable. "We've always been friends—best friends."

No way. Megan pushed his hands away and stepped back. "We might have been friends once, but we aren't anymore."

Megan stared past the seven empty pint-sized ice cream containers lined up on the coffee table. They obscured the view of the talk-show host while he interviewed Billy—Alec—Daniel—she wasn't sure which

Baldwin sat in the hot seat of the late-night show, and she didn't really care. In her ice cream induced stupor they all looked the same.

It didn't matter. Nothing really mattered anymore.

One empty container for every relationship Jack had ruined. Greg, who would only eat premium, brand-named ice creams; Andrew, who only ate straight chocolate, not Dutch chocolate or chocolate fudge, only plain chocolate; Michael, who microwaved his because he didn't like to eat his ice cream frozen; Jerry, who didn't even like ice cream; Kevin, who smothered his ice cream in any and every topping known to man along with tons of whipped cream; Steven, who didn't care what kind or flavor of ice cream it was, he ate it all; and then Brandon, who never got a chance to have ice cream with her.

And Jack had stepped between Megan and whatever boyfriend she'd had at the time . . . for her own good.

Her own good?

Who was he to decide for her? Megan looked from one to the next and the next and the next empty carton. She only then realized that if it had not been for Jack, she might still be with any one of them, wasting her time on a relationship that would never work.

Jack might have been right about those guys, all those guys, but he still was wrong in doing what he had.

There was one good thing to come out of this mess. With the six cartons Jack had pulled out earlier and the seven she'd cleaned up now, at least her freezer was empty.

Jack sat at his kitchen table, lifted the lid on the black velvet box, and stared at the engagement ring he'd intended for Megan.

He'd wanted to impress her, wanted everything to be perfect. He snapped the box closed and pressed it to his forehead, squeezing his eyes shut.

When had everything gone wrong?

Who was he kidding? When had anything gone the way he wanted?

He'd had no right, no right at all, to meddle in Megan's life. He knew it. He wasn't her father, big brother, or boyfriend, and at this point, he wasn't even her friend.

By now Jack's salad, sitting in the refrigerator, had lost its crispness, the once-melted cheese topping on the lasagne had hardened, and the garlic bread sat on the counter untoasted. The hand-packed gelato sat frozen in the freezer. It would keep like that for a long time.

So would Jack's heart. It felt frozen . . . and it would take a very, very long time, if ever, before it would soften and he could love anyone again.

Jack pulled open the ring box and started at the emerald-cut diamond set in a filigree platinum band.

All Jack had wanted was for Megan to say yes. And the way things had turned out, he'd never gotten the chance to ask her the question.

Chapter Sixteen

The following day at work, Jack stared at the spiraling motion of the screen saver, changing colors through red, yellow, green, and blue while altering its shape as it tumbled across his computer monitor.

The phone rang. "This is Jack," he answered.

"Am I going to be a brother-in-law yet?" It was Eric Donnelly.

"You're asking the wrong guy. I'd be the very last person to know."

"I swear, that girl," Eric grumbled.

"*Woman,* please."

"Females." Eric exhaled, exasperated. "Can't live with them, and who'd want to? Sometimes they make life miserable."

"*I* happen to be in love with her. I can see why she's angry that I butted in on her life, but I was doing it because you asked me to, and it got me into trouble."

"So it's my fault?" Eric's feigned shock didn't even sound close to convincing. "I like how you turned it all around."

"*You're* the one who wanted me to act the big brother. Don't you remember? 'You've got sisters—you know what it's like, Jack.'" He did his impersonation of Eric. "'Keep an eye out for her, Jack.' 'Don't let any creep near my little sister, Jack.'"

"She *would* take your help as an insult." Eric was doing his best to deflect the blame, but it wasn't going to work. "You're not supposed to *tell* her you did it. Women take all that honesty stuff seriously, you know. You've got to keep it subtle with them, be one step ahead."

"As if I could ever outsmart her." Somehow Jack had known there'd be a day when he'd have to come clean. "By the way, when did *you* learn so much about women?"

"I photograph supermodels all day, and I think they fall under the category of women. If we really want to make a stretch, I'd guess what works on them would work on Megan."

"Oh, no. I'm not taking any advice from you. I'm just going to take care of this my way."

"Your way? You've been doing a great job doing things your way. I understand women's temperaments and how they tick. Don't worry. I'll handle it from now on."

"No, Eric. No." Jack stood, and his voice got louder as his desperation grew. "I really don't think that's such a good idea. Really."

"Don't worry, Jack," Eric said confidently. "I know exactly what to do."

"Please, don't. Eric? Eric?" Jack held the receiver against his ear and closed his eyes.

Could things get any worse?

Megan pulled the top filing-cabinet drawer open. She made space between the *American Federal* file and the *American Foam* file for the *American First* folder.

Maybe she had been overreacting.

Yes, it was true that Jack had interfered in her life, but could she really not forgive him . . . ever? She filed the folder and stood there for a moment, draping her arms on the drawer.

Was pointing out her boyfriends' defects, as Jack had put it, really all that wrong? Last night had felt so unnatural—down was up, and up was down. Nothing she knew, could depend on, was real anymore.

How was she to know that Brandon Wright was married? Married men didn't walk around with a big *M* tattooed on their foreheads, but they usually wore a wedding ring. On second thought, they might not if they didn't want to give away that they were married.

Yes, Jack had been selfish if he'd wanted her for himself, but it had been about her too. He hadn't wanted her to end up with any of the losers she'd been dating. So Jack had been doing her a big favor.

Eric had put him up to it. Jack had admitted that—and that he'd felt bad about doing it. She could hold on to the grudge, or she could get over it and move on.

The one thing she wanted most in the entire world

had happened: Jack was interested in her. It was her wish come true. So how could she walk away from this?

Last night she'd felt hurt and betrayed, and she'd lashed out at him. Would he even speak to her after all those awful things she'd said to him? She'd told him she didn't want to be his friend anymore. That had been cruel, and she hadn't meant it; she was angry.

Life as she knew it could never be the same. Knowing that Jack had . . . feelings for her changed everything. There would be no going back to the way things were before . . . ever.

Part of her was sad that she'd never have Jack as she once had. Things would never be the same between them. That is, if she wanted *anything* between them again. She hadn't decided yet.

Megan had made it through another workday and now faced the hardest part of the day: the evening . . . without Jack. When she arrived home, a package waited for her. The return label said it was from her brother, Eric. She imagined he'd sent it from his current photo shoot location, probably some exotic desert isle.

She left the package and her purse on the kitchen table to change out of her work clothes. Opening a dresser drawer for a pair of comfy socks, she stared at the contents. A good number of her white cotton socks were tinted pink. She pulled open her undies drawer to find more pink panties than she remembered owning— and her once-red undies a considerably lighter shade.

This was Jack's work.

Memories of her first date with Brandon surfaced. She'd walked a half mile in those incredibly uncomfortable shoes that night. Jack had been kind enough to help her out with her laundry.

She had to remind herself of everything Jack had done. Not only had he been kind and helped her at times, he'd also scared off her boyfriends one right after the other—even if it was on Eric's orders.

After changing into sweats, Megan lifted a matching pink cotton top out of the left-hand drawer. Everything except two or three items in that drawer was the same color. Thanks to Jack, all the cotton whites in that load had fallen victim to the red undies. But she'd never hold it against him. It was even too sad to think about. Life without Jack.

Megan wandered into the kitchen and opened the fridge. She wasn't hungry but should think about whipping something up for dinner.

Ginger ale cans lined the left side of her fridge . . . waiting for Jack. He was the one who used to carry her empty cans and bottles out of her apartment before leaving for the night.

He did that for her.

Megan picked up the package from the table. She opened it and pulled out a manila envelope. Inside were some 8×10 pictures and a note: *Remember the good times. The camera never lies. Love, Eric.*

The first photograph was of Shelley Meredith, the bride, with her parents, taken in the back garden of their house. She was beautiful, and a beautiful wedding had followed.

The next photo showed Megan adjusting Jack's boutonniere. At the time, she'd been staring at it, feeling a bit self-conscious that she'd enjoyed the small task so much.

Megan smiled. It had been a nice moment.

Because her attention had been focused on what she was doing, she hadn't seen Jack's face. Tenderness, adoration, and love showed clearly in his eyes, and she, by staring at the rose on his lapel, had missed it. Hadn't someone said that a picture was worth a thousand words?

There had been an odd feeling of closeness when she'd pinned on Jack's boutonniere. When she finished, she'd smoothed her hands down his lapels, feeling his warmth through the gray jacket. Megan didn't know if it had been real or just wishful thinking on her part.

When had Eric taken this? Wasn't he busy taking the family pictures?

The next photo was of Jack and Aunty Max. Both smiling and clearly enjoying each other's company, they beamed affection.

Megan slid the picture to the back of the stack, revealing the next one of her and Jack walking down the center aisle of the church. It looked like a practice run of the real thing. Both looked solemn and formal, bathed in a golden light of serious reflection. Or had Eric used a soft-focus lens?

Next picture, in front of the church. Billy was looking up at Aunty Max. Where had Eric been? How had he managed to take these pictures without being seen?

Next, Billy and his ponies.

Next, inside the reception tent, she and Jack were leaning toward the childhood pictures. Megan's eyes were wide with surprise, and Jack wore a goofy expression. She remembered his saying, "You can't see it there, but we were playing dress-up and all wearing puffy slips and Aunty Max's high heels."

In the next picture, Megan and Jack were dancing. The whole thing had been staged by Eric, and Megan hadn't thought she'd been posing, but Jack had held her tightly against him while they moved to the make-believe music in their minds. Jack had never looked at her that way before. Who would have guessed that a mambo played in the background?

Next . . . this was a flattering one. Megan had her mouth open, and Jack was shoveling in wedding cake with a fork.

She shuffled that picture to the back. Another shot, taken just after the last. Megan wiping the frosting from her lips. The picture had captured Jack's dimpled smile.

The next photo was dimly lit. She and Jack were leaning against each other, their arms draped around the other's waist. Behind them twisted a double line of low lights in the distance.

They looked straight ahead, and the expressions on their faces reflected a couple relaxed and in love.

In love? She and Jack?

Wasn't that what she'd wanted? Wasn't that what she had prayed for? Her resolve collapsed. She didn't want to be angry at Jack. She didn't want to be apart from Jack.

Megan glanced down at the pictures, and a way to re-connect with him came to her.

Thank you, Eric.

She gathered the photos and headed down the hall-way to Jack's place. Megan knocked on the door, said a little prayer, and waited.

Jack left the pile of fortune cookies he'd been munch-ing on at the kitchen table and opened the door. He really didn't care who it was. His eyes shot wide open.

"Do you want to come in?" It felt awkward to ask. They'd never done "awkward" before.

"Yes, thank you." Megan's voice sounded odd, strained.

It shouldn't be this way, not between them. It was wrong. She stepped inside, but she must have felt equally nervous because she wouldn't meet his gaze.

"Eric sent some pictures of the wedding. I thought you might want to see them." She handed him a large envelope.

They eased into the dining room chairs, side by side, and Jack pulled out the photos, resting them on the table. They were wedding pictures, all right. There were photos of his sisters, his parents, and Shelley, who had made a beautiful bride.

There was one of Megan fixing his boutonniere; he remembered that. Had they been alone, he would have tried to kiss her then, but having his parents, sisters, and nieces around had discouraged him.

Him and Aunty Max. It had been good to see her again. Happy, healthy, causing trouble whenever she could.

Him walking Megan down the aisle. He remembered how beautiful she'd looked in that pink dress. *Prophetic* was his first thought, and with his next he shot it down with a mental *fat chance.*

Billy looking up at Aunty Max.

"I think you missed this." Megan pointed at the photo. "That's when Aunty Max told Billy the cereal wasn't for eating."

"That must have bummed him out."

"Only until you got there."

Was it his imagination, or was there a trace of warmth in her response?

Billy and his ponies. That one was suitable for framing.

Next, inside the reception tent, he and Megan were looking at the wall of childhood pictures.

In the next photo, Megan and Jack were dancing. He had held her close and tried his best to "sizzle." *Melting* would have been more accurate. She had felt warm, soft in all the right places, and oh-so-right in his arms.

All the photos showed them during a happy time. How would Jack ever suspect they'd end up the way they were now, completely at odds?

He couldn't tell his parents and Aunty Max what had happened. He couldn't even admit it to himself. Couldn't say it aloud or even *think* it to himself.

"These are great," Jack said.

"I never knew Eric was *this* good. He really makes everyone look photogenic."

Jack slid the front picture to the back.

"Well, almost everyone. I don't think I look so good in that one." Megan tapped the unflattering shot of her, open-mouthed.

By now their heads were close, mere inches apart, side by side, as they stared at the pictures. The warmth of Megan's shoulder pressed into his arm.

It was hard to see what was in the next picture. Jack squinted. He could barely make out a couple backlit by two rows of lights.

Oh. They'd been returning from lighting the lanterns on the driveway. It was after he had kissed Megan. All he remembered of that moment was the high. Never had she felt better in his arms; never had there been a more perfect moment. Everything had felt so right.

"Eric missed my absolute favorite moment," Megan murmured softly.

"He did?" With the slight turn of his head, he discovered she had moved closer. Very close. She was right next to him. "What was that?"

This time she met his gaze.

"This one," she whispered, and she leaned forward, pressing her lips to his in a gentle kiss filled with love and forgiveness.

The kiss ended, and neither one said a word.

Jack kept his eyes closed, afraid if he opened them, he'd find out it hadn't really happened.

"That was my favorite part too," he admitted when he opened his eyes. "It still is."

"I'd be willing to reenact that again for filming purposes," Megan said, smiling. "I'd even be willing to rehearse as many times as you want to get it just right."

This wasn't a dream. It was better than a dream. This was perfect.

"I'm so sorry, Jack. I was angry and—"

He pulled her close. "It not your fault. I thought I was doing Eric a favor by looking out for you. It was a stupid big-brother idea. I shouldn't have listened to him in the first place."

"If you'd told me how you felt, I wouldn't have had to go through that long line of"—she paused—"*gentlemen* . . . when I was looking for someone like you all along."

"Like *me*?" Jack could hardly believe it.

"I've loved you since the day I met you."

That was mind-boggling. "That was-was—"

"A long time ago."

Ten years ago.

Jack picked up one of the fortune cookies and held it out to her. "Open it."

Megan broke open the fortune cookie and read the message inside: *Megan, I love you. Marry me?*

She laughed and glanced at the small mountain of cookies on the table. "How did you know which one to give me?"

"They all say the same thing."

Megan fingered through the loose fortunes piled to one side, and, sure enough, all the fortunes were the same.

"Where's the box?" he muttered to himself. He dug

through the fortune cookies that covered the table, searching for the velvet box. It was here somewhere.

"What's wrong? What are you doing?" Megan asked as fortunes and cookies slid across and off the table.

There!

"Here it is." He dusted off the cookie crumbs and opened the box for her to see inside. "Will you, Megan?"

Megan stared at the beautiful diamond winking in the light.

"Is this too sudden?" Jack kept the ring box in front of her. He wished; he hoped. "*I* don't think so. I'm tired of watching you date the wrong guys, the ones who don't treat you the way you deserve to be treated. It's my turn now. I love you, and I want you to marry me."

"Marry you? Are you kidding?" She gazed into his eyes and decided that he wasn't joking.

This was everything she had wanted—more than she'd wanted. He wasn't talking about just dating but *marrying* him. Megan couldn't imagine life without him. He was her best friend, her everything.

She was making the decision of her life. Megan blinked back her tears and answered, "Yes, Jack." She didn't have to spend any more time looking for a guy like Jack. "You're the one I've wanted all along."